River Sor

ISBN: 978-1-9999658-0-8

www.starnthwaite.uk
Starnthwaite Publishing

River Song

Peter R Sherratt © 2018

My especial thanks to Paul and to Alwyn
for their help and encouragement
and to Alan Mason for his guidance on game-shooting

Frontispiece: The River Gilpin in the Lyth Valley, Cumbria from the bridge at the foot of Rickettrae

Chapter 1

Have you ever sat and watched a river? Have you seen how the water twists and turns, halts in the quiet eddies beside the bank, catches in a branch of the overhanging tree then frees itself and rushes on to catch up with the rest of the stream? It is cathartic is a river. It cleanses the soul. It seems to purify the blood and still the turmoil of the mind as it rushes past, carrying all ills away to leave one washed and purified. In its passing, no moment can ever be repeated. No single droplet of water will ever pass that way again. You can watch it for ever, and then watch it some more.

The sound too is hypnotic, mesmeric, compelling: it burbles and gurgles its song as it bounces across the stones and trips over itself in its headlong rush to oblivion. The babbling brook has a music of its own, a song which finds an echo in the soul. It calls, like a Lorelai siren maiden, her hypnotising voice luring the listener to join her in her watery bed. It draws one on, lulling the senses deeper and deeper into a peaceful repose. I was born beside this river and our lives were inextricably bound together. It was part of me and I seemed to carry its eternal and compelling song within me no matter how far from its banks I roamed. Here was my home.

And so I sat there dreamily, beside the river, half asleep as I watched its passage and listened to its song. It was the end of a long, hot day and I had been working in the forest since sunrise and now, in the twilight, I was happy to rest. I had been a woodsman since I was a child. My mother died when I was six years old and my father, who was also a woodsman, could not leave me alone in the cottage all day, so he took me into the forest with him each day.

I'm sure I was a confounded nuisance initially, rushing round noisily, disturbing the wild-life as well as the peace and quiet of the forest, but I was learning. I would watch father set traps for food; rabbits, pheasants and anything else which offered itself for our table. Before long, I was able to set my own traps without help and was always proud when our table was adorned by some catch of my own. Over the years I watched carefully how my father worked in the forest. He was patient and would explain every move to me, both before he started and as the work proceeded. As a result, I learned quickly how to be a woodsman and started to help in the work as it progressed.

When I was nine, father bought me a small axe of my own and taught me how to use if safely and effectively. I took huge pride in emulating him in every way. When the sun told midday, we would down our tools and lie on the grass to eat our bait. I would gaze upwards at the tops of the trees waving in the breeze and the sight would lull me; my eyes would start to close and drowsiness come upon me. Just as I was on the point of drifting into sleep I would hear my father's voice. "Come Richard, there is more work to be done".

Each month I would accompany him when he went to collect his wages from the Estate Office and I was well known by the other workers on the estate. Initially they would ruffle my hair and tease me but gradually they came to respect me and recognised that I was making a positive contribution in the forest. Father died when I was thirteen; I continued to work in the forest each day and turned up each month for my wages. I was never formally 'appointed' woodsman in his stead. I was simply accepted and carried on in his place. After all, our section of the forest needed a woodsman to maintain it and I was there and knew what was required and was fully capable of doing the job. Why would they look to appoint someone else?

Like father, I received little in the way of instructions on what was required. From him I had learned what was needed to keep the forest in good order, to promote healthy growth. I knew how to maintain clear bridleways, burn off old heather and control the numbers of pests such as foxes. I had learned how to think like a woodsman and was diligent in my duties.

A section of the forest had been allocated to father many years before and, by default, I inherited that section and continued to work it, following his death. Apart from on the occasional shoot, no one ever went there so no one ever saw it. And yet, personal pride dictated that I preserve and maintain my sector in pristine condition. I would tolerate nothing less than perfection and spent my entire life maintaining it in that state – for my own satisfaction.

No tree ever fell in my part of the forest but I knew about it and would deal with it quickly and effectively. Diseased trees and bushes were quickly grubbed-out and burnt. Any foxes trying to start new earths were quickly discouraged. I understood and nurtured the wildlife less able to care for itself. As a result, the forest was alive with wildlife, all around me. In addition to the pheasants, partridge and grouse, other edible game included rabbits galore and the occasional hare. There were red deer and roe deer, there were wild pigs and boar. I felt no shame in allowing the bounty of nature to feed me at my table.

In addition to edible game, the forest teemed with wildlife of every variety; weasels, stoats, otters, badgers, foxes to name but a few. One had only to stand still in the forest and listen and look, to become aware of the wealth of wild life all around one.

My cottage; the cottage father had built; was near an island in the river, just where the river turned eastwards. It was a tranquil spot with a weeping willow bathing its branches in the still water beside the bank. I had experienced little of riches or glamour and to me this quiet acre of ground was a small part of the Garden of Eden. I loved it and had no need or wish for anything greater. I would be happy to live and die in this paradise beside my river.

My nearest neighbour, one of the Estate's river bailiffs, had a cottage about two miles downstream and I rarely saw him. It was a quiet life and one needs to be 'self-sufficient' to survive both mentally and physically as a woodsman. I grew my own vegetables in a patch of land I had cultivated. I usually visited the market in town once each month to obtain essential supplies; one or other of the gamekeepers might pass through my section of the forest a few times each year and there would be gatherings of estate workers at Harvest time and at Christmas. Apart from that, and collecting my wages each month I would often not see another living soul for months on end.

And I liked it that way.

I had been particularly busy in the forest over the past week or two. A massive storm had brought down a whole stand of trees across one of the bridle paths a fortnight back and I needed to deal with them to clear the passage and to promote new growth. The felled trees needed to be logged and stacked to provide winter fuel for the Estate. I had been working long hours and, on this particular evening, felt tired and weary as I sat, dreamingly watching the stream.

It was hot and sunny; and bees and other insects buzzed lazily in the humid evening air. I was sitting on a comfortable bench outside my cottage having just eaten a large and very satisfying meal of rabbit stew and, yes, I was feeling sleepy. The sound of the brook and the passing of the water were mesmeric, soporific. I was on the verge of dozing into a delightful snooze. I was at peace with the world and the world was peaceful.

It couldn't last. My reverie was shattered by shrieking and screaming from further up the river.

"Help! Help! Stop it. Quick, get it. Help!"

I was awake in a trice and on my feet, just in time to see a bundle being borne along on the fast-flowing current. Having no clue what was going on, I leapt into the stream and grabbed the bundle as it flew past.

It was a mistake and I should have thrown it back immediately. It was a baby in some sort of basket. I looked at the tiny thing for a moment and the only thought which came to my still-drowsy and befuddled brain was the stupid thought,

"You must be Moses."

At that instant, a young woman came tearing into view, breathless and crying.

"Oh! Thank you, thank you," she sobbed over and over again as she checked the sodden bundle. "You've saved my baby."

Well, I suppose I had. Though whether I would have done so if I had thought about the consequences, I'm not too certain.

So, here I am beside the stream with a girl, holding a bundle of baby. The first thing I notice about her, the girl that is, not the baby, after I take my eyes off her heaving and very attractive chest, is that she is very pretty, slim and rather young. Probably not more that eighteen to twenty years old. Concentrating to keep my eyes on her face, rather than elsewhere, I led her to the bench and sat her down, before I went to fetch her a cup of water. She drained it quickly and I refilled it for her. The chest was still bobbing up and down rather quickly, but she was obviously regaining her composure.

She thanked me again and again and then, as I probed, started to unfold her story. She had been 'sweet in the hay' with a local farm boy last autumn and had fallen pregnant after only a few liaisons. She had hidden the fact from her widowed father but could no longer hide it when the baby was born a couple of days ago. Her father had gone berserk and thrown her out of the house. When she tried to return, he had thrown the baby into the stream, several miles above my cottage.

As I chronicle this history with the benefit of hindsight, I recognise that this was a defining moment which was to dictate the entire course of my life, thereafter.
So, pause, gentle reader, reflect and advise me how I should have proceeded from here.

I asked if she had eaten recently and she told me that she'd had nothing since the baby arrived. I had some food left on the hob from my own meal and offered her a plate. She consumed it ravenously and even asked for more. By this time, the baby was crying and, without ceremony, she bared her very attractive bosom and fed the infant.
That was a tough moment.

When the bairn was satisfied, she took it across to the stream and washed it before begging some linen of me in which to wrap it up again. She washed the soiled wrappings in the stream and I again thought how fortunate it was that the stream carried away all ills.

Dusk was beginning to gather by now and it occurred to me to enquire what her plans were. A foolish question! There weren't any.
"I have nowhere to go," she said as she reverted to sobbing.
"Can I stay here?"
"What?"
"Only for tonight. Please!"
"But this is a one-bedroom cottage. There is only one bed."
"I don't mind, if you don't," she sobbed. "I'll be ever so quiet."
She may have been quiet, but the baby wasn't. It woke every few hours throughout the night and totally annihilated any semblance of sleep. This made me frighteningly aware of the soft, warm and very desirable body lying next to me in

the bed. It was all I could do to stop myself putting my arm round her and I slept very little that night. Both girl and baby were asleep when I finally conceded defeat, rose, dressed and left the cottage.

I took my axe from behind the kitchen door and stumbled off into the forest in a daze. Thank goodness it was only for one night. I did my best to concentrate on my job. I had a clear plan of the area I was working on; which trees to clear, which to leave. Halfway through the morning I stood back and looked. I knew I had got it wrong. I got back to work and concentrated hard and did my best to sort out the mess I had made. I had brought some bread and cheese for my lunch and ate it in the silence of the wood before getting back to work.

The sun told me when the working day was over and I made my way wearily back to my cottage, longing for some peace – and some sleep. She was still there.
"Well, I had nowhere else to go so I thought if I cleaned your cottage and made a meal for you, perhaps you would let me stay another night," She said.
"What?"
"By the way," she said, "My name's Mary."
"Oh! Hello Mary," I said, trying to be civil. "I'm Richard."
"Well come and sit down, Richard, your dinner's ready."
And, if I'm honest, her cooking was better than mine.

After dinner she told me to take my ease and she did all the household chores, as well as attending to the baby each time it demanded attention. I was weary and just let it happen.
Darkness fell and we repaired to the meagre bed together again. Despite my fatigue, I was even more aware of her presence that night than I had been previously. I tried hard to concentrate on sleeping but was profoundly aware that there is something wonderfully soft and lovely about a slim young woman. It took me an age to fall into a fitful slumber,

disturbed as before by the regular feeding demands of her baby.

Again, I awoke early and left the cottage before either Mary or her baby was astir. I worked hard to concentrate on my tasks and made some good progress that day. As a woodsman, I regularly set traps and that evening carried home a pheasant and two rabbits for my pot. Somehow, I was not surprised that Mary was still there. Although there had been nothing in the cottage to cook for dinner, she had the pot boiling and had collected some herbs. She expertly jointed the rabbit and had it in the pot before I sat down and it was not too long before she had dinner on the table. It was delicious. Moreover, the cottage was spotless. I could happily have managed without the baby but, apart from the minor issue of sleep, I had little to complain about.

It's a strange thing about life that you do not necessarily remember the point at which a situation became established or accepted but, by then, it is too late: there is no way back. That's how it was. I never, ever said 'yes'. I think I just forgot to say 'no'. And so the pattern established itself. Each night when I returned, she was there. She looked after me with infinite care and concern. Yes, the baby's needs had to be attended to, but she made very sure that I lacked for nothing. The bounty of the forest that I brought home from my traps each day would appear on the table next evening, deliciously prepared. If I lacked for anything – apart from sleep - I have no idea what it was. Indeed, I was enjoying her company and her chattering conversation. My world had changed.

A few nights later, fatigue overtook me and I slept long and deep. I awoke to find that, either consciously or subconsciously I had put my arm around her in my sleep. She had not resisted. After the birth of the baby she was not initially able to respond to my embraces in bed. However, before too long, that problem passed and we became more intimate. It was at that stage in our relationship that I was totally lost in her arms and, if she had asked me to walk on water, I would have done my utmost to comply. She was lovely. I had never had occasion to learn how soft and warm and sweet the lips of a young woman could be; her body was welcoming beyond belief.

There is not a huge amount of worldly wealth in being a woodsman, but the forest is bountiful and provided food for us each day. Some supplies, such as flour, butter and salt and clouts for the baby, could only be obtained from the local market. I was in the habit of making the trip each month and asked if she would like to join me. She told me that her father regularly visited that market. She had no wish to come face to face with him and preferred to stay in the cottage. So, I went to town alone to stock our larder and the baby's growing needs. Whilst I was there I negotiated with a traveling tinker to buy a bolt of material for Mary to make clothes for herself and for the baby.

By now, the bairn – she called him John – was growing fast. Mary said he needed more milk than she could supply so I humoured her by buying a goat. Sure enough, she milked the goat each day and John was weaned onto goat's milk, meaning that her delightful bosoms were left to my sole attention. John was welcome to his goat's milk and Mary took to making cheese with any milk that was left over.

Mary was brilliant in the kitchen. Beside my nightly fare, she regularly baked fresh bread and made most wonderful pies with the meat left over from our meals. It was an especial treat to include a pie in my bag for my lunch in the forest.

Before she died, Mary's mother had taught her to read and write: something I had never learned. With infinite patience Mary started to teach me the skills and, each evening, after the baby had been put to bed, she would devote time to helping me recognise and form the letters. I was a poor student but she would not give up and gradually, so gradually, I started to put words together. Then, quite suddenly, I got the hang of it, it all made sense. I practiced each evening and, ere long, became quite skilled

Mary took-over the management of the small vegetable garden near the cottage. She grew a variety of food for our kitchen. No weed ever dared to trespass there but fresh vegetables seem to spring regularly from the ground to greet her as she passed by.

As planned, she also set-to with the material I had bought for her and a few days later, she and the baby were attired in matching outfits. She even made a new shirt for me from the material. I was quite touched.

And so we settled into a comfortable routine. She no longer asked if she could stay another night and I stopped wondering whether she would still be there when I returned from my day's work.

Chapter 2

I sat on the bench one evening after a pleasing meal, listening to the song of the river and watching as the water changed colour with the setting of the autumn sun over the mountains of Cumberland. The shadows slid silently through the valleys, accentuating the contours of the land, gradually enveloping the foothills in deepening shades as they climbed higher and higher until only the tips of the hills were illuminated with a glow from the last rays, the dying embers of the sun before its departure cast the entire world into the gloom of on-coming night. The crescent moon was already clearly visible and pinpricks of stars were starting to adorn the heavens. It was beautiful.

As I sat there contemplating the loveliness of nature, it occurred to me that Mary was trying to change me. Why? I didn't want to be changed. But later, I realised that that is how women are. They are never satisfied with what you are. They want you to be something else. For me, this was hard. I became a woodsman because that is exactly what I wanted to be and because of the total peace and quiet. Women, Mary included, were not part of my plan. But here she was, trying to change me.

She had started by tidying up my cottage so that it sparkled like a new pin. I could hardly complain at that except it became clear that if I put anything in the wrong place, it was immediately restored to its proper place. If I entered with muddy boots, my house-clogs would mysteriously appear before me. She was changing my habits of a lifetime.

She was teaching me to read and write. I wanted to be able to do that so I could hardly complain at that. She was making me more aware of my appearance, smartening me up and making me more presentable; darning my clothes as soon as a hole appeared. I couldn't complain at that. But it went on and on: my eating habits, cleanliness and so on. I was being organised, changed, bit by bit. I was not used to such close attention and found it rather disorientating.

She made me parade possible options for my future before her; why be a woodsman all your life? Gamekeeper, gillie, pheasant breeder and a number of other options which had no discernible name, were discussed. I was sent to see the Laird. I was not certain why he was always addressed as 'the Laird'. Our Estate was in England but it was close to the Scottish border. Many years later, I learnt that both Cumberland and Westmorland had been part of Scotland at the time of the Norman Conquest. Perhaps that was the reason for our use of the title.

I don't think he had been aware of my existence until that stage, but he received me kindly enough. He was a similar age to myself and I found him both charming and likeable and we had a long conversation.
What did I do, where did I work? What experience did I have?
I think I surprised him on this last point as I was immensely aware of what went on in the forest. I knew more than his gamekeepers and gillies were telling him. I told him where I lived, near to the island in the middle of the stream, just where it turned eastwards. He promised to ride over on Sunday for a longer discussion.

He arrived on Sunday afternoon, as promised, accompanied by his river gillie, David Marshall. Mary had made certain that the cottage was immaculate and our visitors were impressed when they entered. She gave each of them a refreshing cup of her elderflower cordial and they thanked her. We talked for a long time and he probed my knowledge of his estate and of country lore. At length, he offered me a job as an assistant game-keeper on his estate, a big step-up for me. Mary was delighted until I suggested that it might be more difficult for me to garner food from the Laird's estate in this new role as part of the job was to preserve the game and protect it from poachers. That evening I sat beside the river and felt that it was travelling too fast for me. But life, like a river, is difficult to slow down.

The head gamekeeper was known as MacTavish and he took an instant dislike to me. He made it plain that he did not approve of the Laird's decision to promote a mere woodsman to the elevated position of assistant gamekeeper and he worked hard to make my life as miserable as possible. Fortunately, there were several other assistant gamekeepers scattered at various points through the forest, all of whom were subject to his ire, and I struck up a particularly close friendship with one of them. His name was Mitch and he spent many hours accompanying me on my rounds, teaching me the ropes and instructing me in the do's and don'ts of game keeping. We became firm friends and he often called in at our cottage at the end of the day. I noticed that it was generally around suppertime; but Mary was happy to feed him and never complained. She knew that he was helping me enormously.

Grouse are very considerate and breed themselves quietly up on the grouse moors without help from humans. Pheasants and partridge are less helpful and, amongst other duties, part of my remit was to breed thousands of their chicks in readiness for the following year's shooting season. Over time I came to loath the confounded creatures. However, guided by Mitch's helpful tuition and advice, I raised my quota and avoided the wrath of MacTavish. I worked hard to maintain a low profile in that direction.

The shooting season ends at the end of January and there is then a scramble to catch the remaining birds, clip their wings so that cannot fly away, and keep a cock pheasant and a cock partridge in an enclosure together with a number of hen birds, to lay eggs. These are then collected and placed under a broody chicken to hatch. Mitch told me that the reason so many chicks were required was that about a third would fall to the guns, a third would be caught by predators and a third would go wild and fly away.

By now John was becoming increasingly active. He was crawling everywhere and was close to walking. We became painfully aware of how tiny the cottage was. It was a two-room, single storey building and it occurred to me that I could construct another room behind our bedroom and knock a doorway through into it.

It was springtime and the evenings were lengthening. Each night, when work was finished, I would spend a little time working on the new room. The floor would be of earth, as was the rest of the cottage. The walls would be stone which was plentiful around the cottage. I had built dry stone walling as part of my work in the forest since my early childhood and I soon had the walls to the appropriate height and looking very respectable. The roof timbers came from the bounty of the forest and the covering was a thatch. We knocked through a doorway and I spent summer evenings lining the walls with mud from the riverbank. I obtained some limestone from a quarry and fired it to break it down. This was then mixed with water to make slaked lime and Mary whitewashed the inside walls of the room. It was bright and airy. I made a small bed for John to sleep on and he moved into his new room. That night we celebrated having the room to ourselves when we retired to bed.

I needed to visit the market to purchase some items I required. On this occasion Mary agreed to join me and she brought John along too. She had a long list of items she needed and I left her to peruse the wares on the various stalls whilst I went about my own business. When I emerged from the store there was a noisy skirmish taking place in the square. I could not see Mary so quickly pushed my way through the throng to look for her. She was in the middle of the fray. John was lying on the ground screaming. A stranger was repeatedly beating Mary with a stout stick and she too was crying out for help. No one moved to help her. I pulled him off her and span him round. He was a big fellow, but he hadn't spent years wielding an axe in the forest. I knocked him out cold with one single blow. He fell to the ground and didn't move. There was a leather bucket beside the horse-trough. I filled it with water and poured it over him. He came to; I hauled him to his feet, told him that if he ever laid a finger on my wife again, he was as good as dead. I then chased him out of town to the applause of the crowd as I scourged him soundly with the stick he had used to beat Mary.

Mary had picked John up by this time and was trying to comfort him although she was still sobbing herself. We cuddled together, there in the market place until all the tears were dried. Mary was feeling rather battered and bruised it looked as though her arm was broken. I knew that there was a medicine woman in the town, and sought her out. She was a wizened old woman and, in former times would almost certainly have been classed as a witch. However, she seemed to know what to do. She bound Mary's arm in a splint of wood and gave her some medicine which she said was extracted from the bark of the willow tree. It was not unpleasant and seemed to easy Mary's obvious discomfort.

Mary limped a little as I led her into an inn across the square so that we could sit and recover.
"What did you call me?" She asked as we sat down at a table. In the heat of the skirmish I had not paid too much attention to what I had said, but she was clearly thrilled that I had referred to her as 'my wife'. Country folk in our remote part of Cumberland rarely bothered with getting 'churched' in those days; they couldn't afford the services of a parson. They just carried on living together and no one fretted about it. Although I had given the matter no thought, she was undoubtedly 'my wife' and the episode had welded us more firmly together.

"By the way," she continued, "I expect you guessed that that man was my father."

We spent the afternoon purchasing all our needs. I had a little money saved up and squandered it on some books to further my learning. Back at the cottage I absorbed them eagerly and read each one several times over. I found I had a thirst for knowledge and purchased more books whenever the opportunity presented itself.

It took Mary's arm almost two months to heal and I had to render additional help to enable her to do many of her daily chores about the cottage. Gradually, however, nature took its course and the break healed and life returned to normal.

John was now a year old and had been in my cottage since he was two days old. Strictly speaking, he may not have been my son, but it was impossible not to be captivated by him. He was an engaging little fellow, normally full of smiles and laughter and I spent many hours playing with him. I made him some simple wooden toys but his favourite was a wooden stick which he used to bang things with; the noise delighted him. Mary always referred to me as 'daddy' when speaking to him and it was a special thrill when he rose to his feet one day, held out his hands and walked seven or eight steps towards me saying 'dada'. There was a lump in my throat as I caught him before he could fall. We were 'family'.

I was summoned to see the great MacTavish. He told me in very officious tones that there was to be a shoot in my sector of the forest in about six weeks' time. I was to plan and organise the shoot, hire and organise the beaters, keep records of the game shot and organise its sale. I was to be careful to ensure that the gun dogs were properly trained and to attend to the cleaning of the guns after the shoot. In the meantime, I was to be particularly vigilant for poachers. As always, he made it clear that he perceived me as totally incompetent and merely warned me to minimise the downside of my failure. In short; not encouraging.

I immediately sought out Mitch for advice on how to proceed. He was much more helpful and went through the process, point by point. He gave me a comprehensive list of known beaters and pointed out their strengths and weaknesses, and those of their dogs. He schooled me carefully in all aspects of the shoot and how to make it a memorable experience for the participants. I noted his every word and, over the next few weeks, worked feverously to ensure that every aspect was perfect.

The weather helped. It was not too sunny and not too wet – just perfect. The birds obliged. It was not a question of whether there would be sufficient game; the problem was trying to avoid stepping on the blighters as one walked along. The dogs behaved impeccably and none of the guns tried to shoot their owners in the foot. In short, it was a raging success. The bag was enormous and the Laird made a special show of coming up to me at the end to congratulate me on the best shoot in years. MacTavish glowered in the background and growled that the guns could have done with more ground-cover to conceal them. They say that you can't please all the people, all of the time. It's true! None-the-less, I generously thanked MacTavish for his advice, and guidance. Creep!

By tradition, on our estate, the gamekeeper gets to keep a proportion of the bag and also receives tips from the guns. These were generous and I was proud to share them both with Mary. She was able to purchase much-needed items for all of us with the proceeds. A successful day!

Indeed, the success of that day did no end of good for my reputation and for my standing with the Laird. Whenever we met he would call me over for a chat, he consulted me on forthcoming events in the forest and regularly drafted me in to assist with other shoots where they were clearly short-staffed. He was invariably courteous and kind.

One time when we met he called me over.

"Richard!" he had addressed me as such since our first meeting. "David Marshall is the Water Bailiff on the stretch of river near your cottage. He's been taken ill and is likely to be off for some time. Do you think you could cover his duties as well as your own whilst he's away?"

"I'd be delighted," I replied. "But may I ask a favour in return. Since you very kindly appointed me as an assistant game keeper, there has been no woodsman to tend my sector of the forest. I still do a little work there in my spare time to ensure that the bridleways are kept open, but it's beginning to get a little wild again and it hurts me to see it becoming overgrown. Do you think you could find someone to replace me as woodsman?"

"I'll see what can be done. In the meantime, go and visit David and learn what is required." And with that, he rode off.

I went to visit David at the earliest opportunity. I knew him, of course. As I mentioned, his cottage was a couple of miles down-river from mine and he had often passed my cottage on his patrols of the river, but he was a changed man. He was clearly very ill and it occurred to me that it would be some time before he was back on his beat.

We spent a long time chatting and he taught me a great deal. He clearly loved his trade and loved his river. He talked me right along the river, stretch by stretch. Which bits were shallow, where the water ran deep, where the branches of trees could cause a danger of damming the river; where the fish lay and where they made their redds and spawned; parts of the river to keep an eye on in certain weather conditions and which at other times. He told me of the pattern of patrols he followed and how and when he varied it and, finally, he warned me about poachers who operated with impunity on the river.

I absorbed all his instruction and called upon him again many times that season to check on additional information and keep him informed.

When the Laird had mentioned the idea of amalgamating the two roles, it had sounded an eminently sensible suggestion. The reality was somewhat different. Until his illness, both David and I had worked full-time on our allotted tasks. To try to cover two full-time jobs in one day proved hard. I was up each morn before the lark and Mary was often asleep when I crawled back to bed at the end of the day. She had wanted me to advance, but the price was proving heavy for both of us.

I started my patrols of the river the day after visiting David. David was responsible for eight miles of river banks. That meant that, by the time I returned to the cottage to cover my own duties as assistant gamekeeper, I had already walked sixteen miles each day. It was hard work, but I had always been in love with the river and enjoyed the daily patrol. I got to know that stretch of the river well that year and started to feel and understand its various moods and needs. Having spent years as a woodsman, I was quickly able to spot where trees or flotsam might cause a blockage or flood and dealt with it before it could become a problem. I watched mesmerised at the pools where the fish gathered and was able to catch the odd one to supplement our diet at home. In short, I enjoyed the work as a river bailiff.

The Laird had passed my request for a woodsman to his Forestry Manager who, in due time, sent me a sallow youth of some seventeen summers. His name was Caleb and he was as green as the grass and knew little about the world of a woodsman. However, both his parents had passed away and he had nowhere in the world to go. I was jealous of my section of the forest, so I took him in hand and trained him in how to love and to care for MY forest. I showed him how to build a hut to live in, I showed him how to catch and cook food, I showed him which end of the axe to hold and then I showed him how to care for my precious forest. I visited him regularly and gradually tutored him in how and what was required of a woodsman. It was slow work.

The time for the annual shoot was fast approaching and I was stretched. Doing David's River Bailiff duties and tutoring Caleb in woodsman-ship left only limited time for my tasks as assistant gamekeeper. Fortunately, I had started rearing chicks early that year and there was no shortage of game. Mitch volunteered to step in to give a hand with organising all the requirements for the shoot and I was grateful for his help.

For some unaccountable reason, poachers seem to prefer working at night. David had warned me that they often appeared on the night of the full moon and had told me of their favourite spot. A full moon was fast approaching and I decided to stake-out their favourite chosen place this moon. I recruited Mitch and Caleb to assist me and we were in position, just before dark. We made ourselves as comfortable as possible, some way from the pool, just where we could observe activity without being seen. We waited for what seemed like an age and were starting to think that we had chosen the wrong night when, quite suddenly, we heard movement ahead of us. There were three poachers and, by the light of the moon, I recognised two of them as men I had seen in the town. They strung a net across the river at the narrow end of the pool. They then moved up-river and walked down in the river and through the pool, herding the fish before them. One of them was carrying a lamp and we were able to watch their progress. They reached the net and, using ropes attached to it, started to gather it around the trapped fish. That was our cue.

I had no wish to capture them as the penalty for poaching was most severe in those days. I merely wanted to frighten them sufficiently that they would think long and hard about repeating their midnight visits. We leaped out of our hiding, making as much of a fearful noise as we could between the three of us. We must have sounded like the devil and all the hosts from hell and the poachers were terrified. They dropped their catch and net and ran for dear life. I had a shotgun which I had acquired for my game-keeping. I fired off two barrels of shot at their retreating backsides and they were gone. I retrieved the net and released most of their catch back into the river; after reserving supper for myself and my two assistants. As we traipsed home I could not help smiling at the thought of our three assailants lying on their beds, having lead pellets picked painfully out of their backsides.

Next morning, I made my way to David's cottage to tell him of the event. There was no response when I knocked and called his name so I opened the door and entered. David was lying on his bed and had obviously been dead for two or three days. I closed his eyes and covered him with the bedclothes then went to seek out the Laird and tell him both of David's demise and also of the poaching. He was sorry to hear about David as he had been a trusted servant of the Estate for many years and he promised to make arrangements for his burial. He then went on to quiz me about the poachers and asked if I had recognised any of them. I lied and said that I had not but told him that I thought they had received such a shock that they would not be returning for a long time.

The Laird said that he would look for a new River Bailiff but asked if I would continue to patrol the river in the meantime. I told him that, with the date of the shoot fast approaching, I was concerned that I was not fulfilling either of my roles to my personal satisfaction. However, I would be happy to oblige until he could find a replacement.

On my next visit to market I was sitting on a bench at the side of the square when I spotted one of the poachers talking to his wife. He left her and headed for the inn, limping slightly. I crossed the square and approached her.

"Mistress," I said, "I see that your husband is limping. Is he well?"

She assured me that he was and that he had merely twisted an ankle and asked why I enquired. I told her that there had been poachers in the forest, two of whom I thought I recognised and that one of my assistants had fired shotgun pellets at the backsides of the retreating miscreants which might have caused them to limp for a while. I reminded her of the penalty for poaching and left it at that. I knew my message would get back to her husband and I was confident that it would be many a moon before he attempted to poach on my part of the river again.

I reduced my patrols of the river to two or three times each week whilst I prepared for the shoot. Mitch was a huge help and took on most of the administrative work of organising beaters and dogs. I sought out Caleb and spent time with him to ensure that that section of the forest was ready for the shoot. He was learning, but not fast enough. I worked out a programme of work to be completed before the day to clear overgrown areas and to make certain that all the bridleways were open. Two or three times each week I took my axe and joined him so that the work could be completed on time. I made a final inspection of the area on the day before the shoot. It was not perfect, but it would pass.

In the event the shoot was again a huge success. The game queued up to be shot and all the guns were delighted with the day's sport. The luncheon was good and the sun shone. The Laird again made a special point of coming across to me to thank me for an excellent day. The guns were most generous with their tips and I took a pocketful of money back to Mary, together with sufficient game to feed our family for a month.

The extra money would prove most welcome as Mary had recently announced that she was pregnant again. This was hardly a surprise as we regularly enjoyed intimacies after retiring to our bed. But this would be special. Much as I loved and had accepted John, this baby would be mine. I made a tiny cot for the baby to sleep in and Mary spent her evenings that autumn and winter making clothes for the bairn.

Mary went into labour on the most atrocious night of the winter. The temperature was well below freezing, the wind was howling round the cottage like a banshee and snow was piled up against the door. I had brought an ample supply of logs inside before the storm started and I managed to keep the cottage warm and dry. Mary was clearly in some pain but we knew that there was no mid-wife within many a mile so we settled down to wait. Towards dawn the contractions came fast and regular until finally she delivered a tiny baby girl. She was still-born. I cleared her mouth and tried to breathe life into her, but it was fruitless. We both cried; me possibly more than Mary. My baby, my daughter was not for this world.

I took the tiny bundle in my arms, took up my spade and left the house. The snow was thinner in the forest and I hacked at the frozen ground until I had dug a tiny grave. I buried the bairn in soil and in my tears and marked the grave so that we could return at a more opportune moment to share our grief.

It took Mary a long time to recover. She was depressed at the loss of the baby and moped about the cottage, listless and miserable. Eventually the snow melted and the spring arrived and slowly she revived. Much later, when she was fully recovered, we tried to make another baby, but sadly, it was never to be.

Chapter 3

John was in his sixth summer and was growing fast. Mary appointed herself as his tutor and had already started to teach him reading and writing. He was a bright lad and quickly cottoned on to the concept. I spent all my spare time playing with him or teaching him more practical skills and here too, he had no difficulty in absorbing knowledge. He was the age I had been when my father first took me into the forest to learn the life of a woodsman and I started to take John out with me when I thought there might be something of interest or a lesson or skill to be learned. John had no one of his own age to play with and rarely saw another human. I started to make a point of taking him into town whenever I went to market, just so that he could learn to relate to other people. On the first visit he stood stock-still in the square with his mouth wide open. He seemed terrified at seeing so many people around him. I sat him in the window of the inn where he could watch and he gradually became more accustomed to the idea that there could be so many people in the world. When he had calmed down, I took him into one of the shops and purchased a book for him to take home and read.

David Marshall had long since been replaced as River Bailiff; Caleb had gradually started to be more of a help than a hindrance as a woodsman and I had time to concentrate on my role as assistant gamekeeper. In the evenings I would sit beside my river and watch it as it bore away all the ills of the world. I was happy with my work; I was happy with my family; I was happy with my life.

As we finished our luncheon one Sunday, I heard the sound of a horse arriving outside. I sprang up and went outside to find the Laird dismounting.

"Richard," he said as he tethered his horse. "Have you time to talk?" I assured him that I had and we made our way to the bench. We sat there in the sunshine for a long time making small-talk. He asked me numerous questions about the forest, the river and how the hatchlings were progressing for the autumn shoot. He asked my opinion on various aspects to do with the Estate. I gave him honest and considered replies on every point.

Finally, he got around to the reason for his visit. The Head Gamekeeper, MacTavish, was ageing. He had recently damaged his leg in an accident and was having difficulty fulfilling his role. The Laird had no intention of dismissing him but was looking for someone to train up and act as overseer and to take over from him when he finally retired. He had been keeping a careful eye on me since I was appointed as an assistant gamekeeper and thought I might be capable of taking on the task. It would mean that I would have to move from my cottage to one of the Estate cottages near to the Estate office and that I would have to take on responsibility for appointing and organising all the assistant gamekeepers as well as overseeing organisation of the various shoots. It was a substantial responsibility. How would I feel about it?

I was both astounded and flattered. This was an unsought opportunity and I said I would need to think about it carefully. I reminded him that MacTavish considered me on a par with earthworms although the Laird protested that MacTavish had gradually changed his opinion as I had succeeded at every task I had been given. We discussed each aspect of the appointment and he was warm in his praise of me and assured me that he thought me fit for the task. Finally, I thanked him and said that I would like to discuss it with Mary before giving a reply. The Laird called a farewell to Mary, remounted his horse and was gone.

Mary emerged from the cottage and joined me on the bench and I related the conversation and offer. She was thrilled and enthused about the opportunity at length. She saw it as a just reward for all the effort I had put in over the years; it was an endorsement of my skill and abilities; it would mean that she would have neighbours to relate to; John would grow up in the company of others; there would be more money for us to live better.

All this was true but I was less enthusiastic. I was born in this cottage; this was MY river; I liked the isolation; I had no wish to be a boss or to organise people and, in truth, we had sufficient money for our needs. I was happy as I was.

I had promised to give the Laird my reply by the following Sunday and, for the entire week, I was assailed unrelentingly by Mary. It quickly became abundantly clear that my life would not be worth living if I turned down the opportunity.

During the week I called upon Mitch. We had developed a good friendship and, if I took this appointment, I would be his boss. I wanted to hear his opinion. Mitch was perfectly relaxed about the change. He felt that he was too old to be in contention and he certainly did not want the responsibility. He was kind enough to say that he thought I deserved the step-up and that he thought I would be good at the job.

On the Sunday, all three of us set out to walk to the Estate Office. It was a journey of several miles but I think I half hoped that Mary would be put off by what she saw. She was not. She enthused about the place, she enthused about the neat row of Estate cottages and, when we were shown into one, she enthused as though it was the most wonderful place on God's earth. It had real stone floors; it had two excellent bedrooms; it had a large kitchen with an inside water pump; it had a separate dining and sitting area; outside it had its own walled cottage garden. She loved it.

I had arranged to meet with MacTavish before giving my reply to the Laird. I wanted to convince myself that I could work with MacTavish and was not there merely as cannon-fodder to make him look good at my expense. In truth, he had aged and the problem with his leg had incapacitated him. He was as near friendly as I could recall and we had a long discussion about the role and how he saw it working. He made it clear that he would be relying heavily upon me to fulfil those parts of the task he could no longer do. In turn, I made it clear that I did not know the role and would be relying on him to tutor me. He conceded that I had proved a quick learner in the past and agreed that he was prepared to help me.

The Laird was not about when I enquired so I left a note for him, confirming my acceptance and arranged with the Estate Office that I would arrive early the following Sunday morning to borrow their horse and cart to move our belongings.

I spent my final week making certain that everything for which I was responsible as assistant gamekeeper was in apple-pie order. I wanted to ensure that, when I appointed my successor, he inherited a patch which was run as I wanted to see it continue. Mary spent the week packing our meagre belongings and preparing for the move. In the evenings I sat on the bench and gazed at my river and listened to its song: I knew that I would miss it.

On Sunday I was up well before dawn and walked to the Estate Office to collect the horse and cart. I walked them back to my cottage and between us we loaded all our worldly possessions onto the cart and were off again, shortly after midday. John was hugely excited and ran backwards and forwards until I had to warn him that he was in danger of being run-over by the horse and cart. I lifted him up and placed him on the cart as that looked like the safer option.

We arrived at our new home mid-afternoon and started to unload our belongings. Mary had worked out in her head where she wanted everything and I left the two of them to do the final arranging and went to return the cart and rub-down and feed the horse. When I returned, all our possessions were where Mary wanted them, the range was lit and supper was already cooking. We sat down to supper together in our new home and I had to admit, somewhat grudgingly, that this cottage was a significant improvement on my childhood home.

The following morning, I reported to MacTavish's office, bright and early, to start my new role. There were seven assistant gamekeepers on our estate and three on an adjoining estate for which he was also responsible. He had a map on his wall and pointed out the various locations as he named them. He told me the incumbents at each location and then went on to share his views on the abilities of each assistant. I was pleased to see that Mitch received a good billing even though he was regarded as 'ageing'. MacTavish wanted me to familiarise myself with all seven men and their parts of the forest. He would continue to manage the adjoining estate for the immediate future.

He had a list of events for the year on his office wall and we went through them in detail. Increasingly, organisation of these events would be my responsibility and I had a lot to learn. We also needed to find a replacement assistant gamekeeper for my patch as a matter of urgency. By their nature, gamekeepers tend to be loners. The presence of Mary in my life was by happenstance; most keepers were unmarried. Similarly, the Estate had found over many years that there was no point trying to recruit from the town. Keepers tended to be itinerant 'loners' and it was largely a case of waiting until some chap turned up, looking for work. They then had to be evaluated to see where they might fit. It could be a slow process.

Whilst we waited for a suitable candidate to appear, I started my visits to each of the assistant gamekeepers. I had met most of them at some point or other in the past but the Estate was vast, covering many thousands of acres and I covered a lot of miles on my visits that year. I visited parts of the

Estate I had not seen before and discovered many breath-taking vistas, beautiful hills and valleys. I felt very privileged to be part of what Mary told me Shakespeare had described is 'this other Eden, demi-paradise'. That seemed to me a most wonderfully apt summation of the glories around me and I immersed myself in the beauty of my new-found surroundings.

I took a bivouac with me on my visits and spent several days at each location. I wanted to get to know the strengths and weaknesses of each assistant gamekeeper. I wanted to understand their locations and what opportunities they offered both for propagating chicks and for the configuration of the various shoots. I needed to know their relationships with the woodsmen in their part of the forest and the interdependencies between the two. With the grand title of overseer, I was entitled to some degree of respect and did, indeed, receive it. Every man was happy to talk about his patch and his ideas for its development. I talked with each of them about forthcoming events and made certain that they had plans in place for each shoot.

Together with reporting back to MacTavish and my growing office-based duties, it took me over a month to complete my visits to all the assistant gamekeepers. However, it was a worthwhile exercise and at the end I felt that I knew more about the Estate, and was much more in control of the situation.

My next task was to familiarise myself with the planning and organisation of events. This was more difficult and was initially outside my comfort zone. Many of the events were annual and had been taking place since time immemorial. These were relatively easy as the arrangements did not vary from year to year. The important part was to ensure that nothing changed. Exactly the same people had to be invited each year and most needed to be housed on the Estate. The same beaters would be summonsed each year and the pattern of entertainments and dining duplicated. In the eyes of MacTavish, omitting an honoured guest from the list of invitees could render one liable to the death sentence so infinite care was required.

One-off events were even more challenging as plans and arrangements had to be developed from scratch. In fairness, it was from involvement in these that I learned most. Over the first few months, my relationship with MacTavish developed well and improved immensely from our former state. He started to rely on me more and more; took me into his confidence and trust. He was more relaxed about leaving things in my hands and we worked well together. It was clear that his own health was fading and the incapacity with his leg was draining him. He recognised that he could no longer do his job without my help.

The income of the Estate came from a number of different sources including farming, forestry, shooting, deer-stalking and fishing. Apart from the farming and forestry, these were the pursuits of the landed gentry and substantial sums of money were involved. The summer months were largely devoted to fishing whilst autumn and early winter was the period for shooting and stalking.

MacTavish introduced me to Matthew Jamison, the Head Gillie. Matthew was in charge of all the river activities and had a number of river bailiffs under his command. By tradition, the Head Gillie and the Head Gamekeeper work together. Their busiest periods do not overlap so that they help each other during the alternate busy periods. MacTavish was no longer able to fulfil his side of the bargain so it fell to me as the overseer to provide the assistance of gamekeepers whilst fishing was at its height. When the shooting season started, the roles would be reversed. Matthew and I took an instant liking to each other and became great friends and this made working together a genuine pleasure.

I was starting to enjoy my new role - but I missed my river!

Chapter 4

Including the servants from the Manor House then depending on how wide one drew the circle, there were fifty or more people living near to the Estate office. Mary and John were ecstatic with their new home and surroundings.

John had friends of his own age to play with for the first time and they roamed wild throughout the forest. At an early stage I had taught him to find his way when lost; be it by the sun, the stars or the direction of north, using the position of moss or lichen on the trees. He was good and we had no fears for his return. I had also taught him how to set traps to capture game and he frequently returned home with food for our table.

Mary too had friends at hand for the first time in her life. She struck-up friendships with a group of wives on the estate and they spent long periods together sewing or organising events or just drinking tea and chatting. She was as happy as I had ever seen her. She continued her daily tuition of John and, at the request of their parents, other children started to join in her 'classes'. One of the other wives worked as a part-time clerk in the Estate accounting house. She was good at sums and added that skill to the lessons for the children's education. Mary also read to the children and encouraged them to read to themselves to widen their general knowledge. John appeared to have an infinite capacity to absorb all that he was taught and was happy to patiently help less-able children to catch up with the rest of the class.

There were endless opportunities for socialising around our new home. Formal events included May Day, Harvest Festival and Christmas parties. But informal get-togethers were just as much fun and on many evenings the men in particular would congregate after supper and chat as the day waned. Sometimes one or other of us would produce a bottle of homemade wine or cider but drunkenness was frowned upon in our society and we drank very moderately.

The Estate had a tiny chapel which dated back to before the reformation. However, it was little used and we rarely saw a parson from one year to another.

At long last, a man arrived on the Estate looking for a job. His name was Jason and he had been an assistant gamekeeper for several years on a well-known estate in the south. The estate was being broken-up and sold piece-meal and he was out of work. I interviewed and quizzed him at length and it was clear that he did know his job. He had brought with him glowing references from his previous employment. I encouraged MacTavish to have a quick chat with him before appointing him and he had no hesitation in endorsing my view.

I accompanied Jason back to my old cottage by the bend in the river. I helped him chase some of the mice and rats from the cottage and arranged to call back a couple of days later to give him a conducted tour of that part of the forest. When I returned, he had already made himself a bed and a stool to sit on and was settling in well. I took him on a tour of his new kingdom and was distressed to see how things had deteriorated in the few months since I had left. I had already agreed with MacTavish that we would not hold a shoot on that patch this year and until Jason had got on top of his job.

I showed him the breeding pens and feed stations for the chicks and the region in which the shoots usually took place. Jason responded intelligently to each situation and I was pleasantly surprised at the depth of his knowledge and experience. I felt that we had found a good man.

I introduced him to Caleb and we agreed a joint programme of work to ensure that they would be ready for a shoot the following year. They appeared to get on well together and I left them to get on with their various tasks, making a mental note to spring a surprise visit in a month or so. I took a long and covetous look at my river and my birthplace and retreated back to my new home.

The fishing season was in full flow and I turned my attention to helping Matthew Jamison, the Head Gillie. On the wall of his office he had a long list of all the fixtures for the year. Some were one-day events. Others were scheduled to last for as long as a week. There was a huge amount of work associated with this. Accommodation and catering had to be organised at the Manor House. Horses and carts were required to take the fishermen to the more remote parts of the river, stands had to be staked out for each rod and water bailiffs had to be organised from all around the Estate to support each fisherman and act as nanny to their whims and moods. Most of the visitors were high-ranking gentry and they invariably included Lords and Earls.

The river beside which I had hitherto spent my life had fish aplenty. However, it was merely a tributary of the main river which ran through the Estate. That was broad and deep and fast-flowing and was a very popular fishing venue. Matthew had been in post for many years and knew his job well. My role was to act as support and to take some of the less skilled drudgery from his shoulders. However, we worked together well and enjoyed the comradery. As the season progressed and I learned what was required, I was able to give greater assistance and be of more use.

The fishing was almost invariably fly-fishing. I had done a great deal of this over the years and prided myself that I was not bad. The ability of the guests varied enormously. Some spent more time trying to remove the fly from the seat of their pants where the hook had lodged during their cast. Others had been coming to the Estate for years and were serious experts. They were a joy to watch. They would stand well into the river and whip the line back and forth, tempting the fish until eventually it pounced and took the bait. They would then play it to weaken its strength until they were finally able to scoop it into their net.

Most of the fish were generally returned to the river at the end of the session. A few larger salmon might be sent up to the Manor House for the guests to dine on that evening or might go to the smoke-house to enable the guest to bear them proudly home at the end of their stay.

I recall one occasion when I was nannying for a famous member of the House of Lords. He was incredibly incompetent and I had already removed the hook from the seat of his pants several times. He finally started to get the hang of the rod and was casting his fly close to the far bank where the water was deeper. There was a sudden movement and the fly was taken. At first, I could not see the fish and it jinked back and forth, trying to release itself but I suddenly realised that it was an enormous pike, fighting for dear life. I called to ask the angler if he wanted help but no, this was his catch and no one else was going to get the glory.

Our guest was rather too far into the river. He was wearing tall leather boots which were waxed and oiled to keep out the water. I could see that, in the course of the fight, the water was already lapping over the top of them.

In fairness, he fought valiantly for twenty minutes or more, but was not really making any progress in trying to reel-in his catch. Suddenly the fish turned and headed in a new direction. It caught the angler totally off balance and he stumbled and fell headlong into the water. He let go of the rod which headed off down the river in pursuit of the pike to which it was still attached.

Our guest was soaked through to the skin. I called one of the Estate workers to conduct him back to the Manor House where he spent the rest on the day huddled round a blazing fire, regaling anyone who would listen about his adventures with a shark – or something. I knew that the rod would eventually snag somewhere or other and headed off down the river and located it several hundred yards away, still attached to the pike. I retrieved the rod and played the catch until it finally surrendered, at which point I carried it back to the Manor House and presented it to our guest. He believed that he had been totally vindicated and continued to exhibit it as 'his' catch. My minor involvement went unmentioned.

For all their exalted positions and apparent pomp, some of the guests were delightful and many were very generous. I saw more gold sovereigns that summer than I had seen in all my life. Some of the lunchtime picnics were very jolly and raucous affairs and occasionally it was a struggle to rouse our guests back to their rods. But they were paying so, whatever they said went.

Matthew Jamison got wind of some potential poaching on the river. The penalty for poaching was very extreme at that time. He organised a stake-out with a dozen of us involved in the exercise and we were in place early on the appointed night. Once again, it was a full moon and the visibility was good. At around midnight we saw six poachers approaching the river near where we were concealed. They started to unload their equipment and to string their nets across the river.

It was at that point that one of our party had a coughing fit, possibly as a result of the tension. The poachers were alerted and started to run, but they were largely surrounded. Most of us had guns and several discharged them at the poachers, two of whom fell, clearly mortally wounded whilst two others had received serious leg wounds and were unable to flee. The party surrendered. Matthew took the names and addresses of the surviving poachers and then instructed those standing to bear home the injured and dead. The survivors would be reported to the sheriff and could answer to him.

I felt that the episode had been rather unnecessarily harsh. But it was Matthew's patch and his call. The law would have exacted similar penalties and it was unlikely that we would be troubled by any of those men again.

Chapter 5

Whilst the fishing season had been progressing, I had been preparing plans for the shooting season, still guided by MacTavish. He was becoming increasingly frail but by now we were firm friends and in those early days, I would not have survived without his input and advice. I shared his office and together we planned each of the shoots which had been arranged.

I made my intended 'surprise visit' to my old patch to see how Jason was getting on. I came across him near the hatchlings feeding post which he was tending and cleaning. I asked him how he was progressing and we had a long chat. He was a true professional and it was quickly clear that he was on top of his job and enjoying the work. He could well have hosted a shoot that season but I felt it would do no harm to give the area a year-off. He told me that he had established a good working relationship with Caleb and they had a clear plan of the forward workload.

With the exception of my old beat, I planned to share the shoot venues equally throughout the estate. I made brief excursions to visit each assistant gamekeeper to ensure that they were ready and had prepared plans for their part of the forest. With minor exceptions, all locations were ready. I ensured that they were aware of the dates and had arranged beaters for the shoot. I spent a pleasant afternoon with Mitch and it was good to relax in the company of my old friend. He asked after Mary and John. His only regret was that, although he had got to know Jason, he couldn't pop in there for his supper as he had been able to do when we lived by the river.

The season always starts with the 'Glorious Twelfth'. I had inspected the grouse moors in advance and selected an area where the old heather had been burnt off two winters back. It was in perfect condition for the birds and the red grouse were there in abundance. The Laird had invited a very select band of guests and they were excited and looking forward to a great day's sport. We started out early and were up on the moor shortly after daybreak. The beaters approached from the opposite end of the moor and the grouse were soon up. There was a cheer when the first grouse was downed and one of the servants was sent to collect it and deliver it to the Manor House where it would be cleaned and cooked in time to join our guests for dinner; properly dressed, of course.

Grouse fly very fast which makes them challenging game but the guns were good. When the party broke for luncheon, the guests were in high spirits. By tradition, they consumed more spirits with their lunch so were in even higher spirits when we returned to the Manor House. The day was declared a major success and the guests celebrated into the small hours.

Following that, we had two more successful shoots although the bag was not as good as it had been on my old patch. I made a mental note to ensure that each assistant gamekeeper was hatching the necessary batches of chicks in future years. By now I knew a number of the guns and they were very supportive of my promotion to overseer and clearly saw me as the future head gamekeeper although I did not relay that back to MacTavish.

The fourth shoot of the season was at the farthest extreme on the Estate. I organised horses and carts to convey the guests to the chosen location so that they would still be fresh when we arrived. The morning went well and the guns had secured a pleasing bag by the time I called a halt for luncheon. The guests gathered round ready for their picnic. Just as everyone started to relax, there was a sudden shot. One guest had omitted to discharge his gun and had managed to shoot his toe off, literally.

The poor fellow was in considerable pain. He had been wearing stout boots but the pellets had gone straight through the leather and amputated his toe. He was clearly in agony and there was no way he could continue the shoot. I cut the mangled remains of his boot from his foot as gently as I could, then had him loaded onto one of the carts and transported back to the house where one of the maids spent a fraught afternoon trying to console him and clean up the wound. I was told that he had got through an entire bottle of whisky. One half went down his throat as an anaesthetic; the other half on his foot to cleanse the wound. Whether from the wounds or the whisky, it was some days before he was able to rise from his bed and hobble on crutches to his coach.

The season is always interrupted towards the end of September by Harvest. Fish and fowl are regarded as part of the Harvest but the Estate yields many other crops beside. In various parts of the Estate corn and similar crops are grown and hay is cut and stored in June or July, ready for when it is needed to feed the cattle in the winter. In addition, a wide variety of other crops are harvested; hard and soft fruit, berries and nuts of every description.

As a result, the Harvest party was always one of the big events of the year. Workers would gather together from all over the Estate to share in a party which was thrown by the Laird as his way of thanking everyone for their work throughout the year. It was invariably held in the Great Barn near the Estate office. Trestle tables and benches would be set up for us all to sit down together at. There was always a great supper to which we were all invited and we would feast until well into the evening. Cider had been made from last year's crop of apples grown on the Estate and a blind-eye was generally turned, should anyone incautiously imbibe a drop too much. There was always someone who could play an accordion or a fiddle and we would sing and dance until we were fit to drop. It was a great occasion and friendships would be made or renewed at the Harvest celebration.

At some point during the evening the Laird usually made a little speech thanking everyone for their work. He had a good sense of humour and usually managed to include a few tales of funny events which had taken place during the year. There would be a bit of barracking, but it was always good-humoured. There would be a few sore heads the following morning but we would all be back at work early on Monday.

After the Harvest celebrations, the shoots continued in earnest. There were generally two or three days' shooting each week somewhere or other on the Estate over the next two months. I was responsible for organising them all and also had to attend each. The Laird attended many of them as host but, in the absence of MacTavish, I was responsible for ensuring that all aspects ran like clockwork. Fortunately, they generally did.

As the shoots circulated to the various parts of the forest it also enabled me to gauge the abilities of each of my assistant gamekeepers. Most were good but a couple gave me cause for concern when the shoots were below our usual standard. The issues were the same at each location. The game was thin on the ground, too few beaters had been engaged and they and their dogs were undisciplined. I discussed my concerns with MacTavish and we agreed a course of action.

The first was an old retainer called Douglas. He had worked on the Estate since he was a lad but, so far as we could work out, was probably getting close to eighty and now lacked the stamina to do a first-rate job. There was no way the Laird was going to terminate his employment and we had to find a way round the problem. One of the Estate families had a son who was about fifteen years old. We interviewed him to see if he might be interested in learning the trade. He was and he appeared reasonably bright. I had the pleasure of taking him out to Douglas's patch and telling Douglas that the lad was to be his apprentice. I wanted him to teach the boy how to be a great assistant gamekeeper over the next few years and, when Douglas felt that the lad was ready to run his patch, the Laird had set aside a cottage for him near the Estate office where he could spend his days as idly as he wished. Douglas had been aware that he was losing his touch but the offer re-kindled his fire and over the next three years he whipped the boy into a very competent assistant gamekeeper before finally making his way wearily towards his retirement cottage where he spent his final years cosseted and cared for by the elderly matrons of the Estate. It was a good outcome all round.

The second assistant gamekeeper was in his first full season on the Estate. A lad who gloried in the wonderful old English name of Dale Watler. We agreed that I would spend time with him to help him understand what was required and to coach him in how to achieve the required results. We would give him the benefit of the doubt and watch for improvements over the next twelve months. I did as agreed and made regular visits to mentor the lad. The youngster flourished. He quickly assimilated the task, the requirements and the road to achieving them. By the end of his second season he was up there with the best of them and I was proud of his progress. Again, a good outcome.

The red grouse season ended about the middle of December but most other game continued in-play until the end of January. First, it was time for the Christmas celebrations.

By tradition, the Laird invited everyone on the Estate to call at the Manor House on Christmas morning. There were little presents for the children and a dram or two for the parents. We would stand around the huge Christmas tree and sing traditional ancient Christmas carols. Afterwards we would process to the Great Barn near the Estate office, still singing carols and in high spirits. In the barn a Christmas luncheon had been prepared and we would sit and eat and drink until it fell dark. Those responsible for the cattle would gradually drift off to milking; the rest of us continued until bedtime. It was a wonderful occasion.

I sat there beside Mary and we talked about how our life had changed this year. John was running around with his friends, as happy as a child can be. Yes, it had been a good year for us and the move to overseer had brought prosperity and friends.

I still missed my river and I longed to hear again its song; but times were good.

Chapter 6

That winter, it rained.
It rained and it rained and it rained.
And, just when one knew it could not possibly rain any more, it did.
It rained and it rained and it rained.

The ground was sodden. Everywhere was sodden. Everything was damp.
Mould formed on everything in the cupboards and most things in the house.
I wore my tall leather boots every day for almost two months and it rained and it rained and it rained. Huge areas of the Estate flooded. And then the river burst its banks.

That was serious. Our livelihoods depended on it. With an army of workers from the Estate, I patrolled the river, trying desperately to shore-up banks in danger of collapse. We failed and thousands of acres of our precious land were under water.

Fish flapped around on the forest floor, desperate for the main stream; thousands of just-hatched young chicks were drowned and washed away. It was heart-breaking. The hides were flooded, the cottages were flooded, the world was flooded and there was nothing we could do about it.

Of course, it stopped eventually but, by then the damage was done. The one sensible thing I had done during the rains was to make careful sketches of the points at which the river had breached its banks. That spring an army of Estate workers spent hundreds of hours shoring-up those weak points to reduce the likelihood of flooding next time it rained like that.

It took months for the Estate to recover. Matthew had to cancel most of the early fishing parties and, even later in the season, he was still complaining that things had not returned to 'normal'.

By the time the shooting season opened, things were starting to dry out but the flooding had killed thousands of chicks which should have joined the shoot. It was heart-breaking, but we survived.

As the year progressed we celebrated. We celebrated May Day, we celebrated Harvest, we celebrated Christmas. We were heartily sick of that year and eagerly awaited the next. With each celebration, the wheel turned and I was suddenly surprised to realise that I had been overseer for four years and that John was nearly ten.

MacTavish was becoming increasingly infirm and, through the period of the floods, he rarely left his bed. One night I was awakened from deep slumber by shouts of 'Fire! Fire! Fire! MacTavish's house was ablaze.

I leaped from my bed to join in the effort to stem the blaze but it had a good hold by then and we wasted our efforts. The roof and timbers burned away to nothing, leaving only the shell. We conjectured that he had probably gone to sleep with a candle burning. The flame had caught onto the bedclothes, MacTavish would have suffocated quickly and the house burned down around him.

The following morning the Laird came to inspect the damage which was severe. It had been a substantial house and he immediately gave instructions for it to be rebuilt. Nothing could be done for poor MacTavish and the fire had destroyed all trace of his earthly remains. Later, we all traipsed along to the chapel where the Laird said some nice things about the man and that was that. He was gone.

From my initial dread of MacTavish, our relationship had gradually developed into a friendship and I had learned a huge amount from him. Now I was alone and had no one to rely upon except myself. I was the sole occupant of his former office and could not turn to him seeking endorsement of my plans. I was on my own.

Nonetheless, he had taught me well and I found the strength and courage to face every problem, every situation. The year continued to turn, the plans and arrangements still had to be made and I found that I was equal to the requirements. I assisted Matthew through his busy period on the river and, in turn, he aided me during the busiest moments of the shooting season.

Mary wanted to arrange a party to celebrate John's tenth birthday. She planned that, with some of the other mothers, she would take the children to a well-known beauty spot deep in the forest. I had a shoot on that day so could not join them but I organised a horse and cart to take them on their journey, before I left for the day. My day went well and I hardly gave them another thought.

The Laird had not joined the shoot that day and so I was surprised when, later in the afternoon, he rode into our midst.

"Richard," he said. "A moment of your time."

We walked over to the side of the clearing before he continued.

"Richard, if there is an easy way of telling you this, I do not know what it is. There has been an accident. Mary is dead, killed by a wild boar. Go home and comfort John; I will see to the rest of today here and we will talk later."

I was speechless, numb. I did not even acknowledge that I had heard what the Laird had said. I turned and left. In shock I stumbled my way back to my cottage where I found a neighbour trying to comfort John. I thanked her and she left and when she had gone I gathered John into my arms and, holding each other, we sat and cried and cried. It was past dark when we finally parted. I cut some bread and cheese for him and when he had eaten it, packed him off to bed where I hoped that fatigue would carry him into healing sleep.

Then I went to find a neighbour who could give me an account of what had happened. The party had been in full flow with happy children playing and whooping with delight. Quite suddenly, a wild boar had appeared on the scene, attracted by the noise and had made to attack some of the children.

Mary had picked up a stout stick and interposed herself between the boar and the children to protect them. The boar had paid no attention to the stick and had charged at her. She had stood her ground so that the boar concentrated on her, rather than the children who scattered in every direction. The force of the impact had probably killed her instantly but, not satisfied, the boar had then proceeded to gore her body with its tusks. Without weapons, there was nothing anyone could do.

When the boar had satisfied its anger, it wandered off into the forest again. Other parents had lifted Mary's body onto the cart and the party immediately made its way home. They had laid Mary's body in the chapel and I took a lantern and went to say my farewells to her. I lifted the mantle which had been placed to cover her. She was a sorry sight and I vowed that the boar would die.

The following morning I took John with me and he helped me to dig a grave at the edge of the forest. As we were finishing, the Laird rode up and he helped me to carry Mary's body and place it in the grave. He then took the initiative and said some nice words over the body. He talked about her as a wife and a mother and as a person; then he went on to say some church words to help her up to heaven. We covered her body with soil, marked the spot with a little wooden cross and John and I made our way back home.

The following day I left John in the care of a neighbour and I went back to my old cottage beside the river. With Jason's agreement I sat on the bench outside the cottage and watched the river until it got dark. It seemed to sing a sad song to me that evening as the twilight gathered. The shadows told only that Mary had departed. The river had brought her to me and in my mind I released her spirit back into the river to travel onwards.

A few days later I took my shotgun and some heavy ammunition and retraced the journey of the children's party back into the forest, with murderous intent. I knew what boar droppings looked like and searched that area of the forest looking for tell-tail signs. It took me a long time to find traces of the beast but, when I did, it was quite sudden. Almost at the same moment as I found the traces, I also heard the beast and it was quite close. I readied my shotgun and tentatively peered round a large holly bush. It was there. It was enormous and it fitted the description I had been given that one of its tusks was deformed.

I should have shot and killed it from there but some stupid sense of fair-play prevailed. Instead I made a noise and threw a stick at it. It was not amused, it rose and came tearing towards me like a bat out of hell. I ducked behind a tree and it went careering past me. It came to a halt, turned and looked at me from twenty yards away. Again it charged and I fired one barrel of the shotgun; still it came on and I discharged the second barrel. It did not appear to slow but continued its deathly charge at me and then, quite suddenly, collapsed and fell at my feet, inches away from what would have been my certain death.

I stood there shaking, half way between elation and abject fear. I had been incredibly stupid in alerting the beast.

Another second of life, a few more inches of travel and I would now have been on my way to join Mary.

It was enormous and must have weighed as much as two or three grown men. I made a hurdle of branches, rolled the beast onto it and hauled it back to the Estate office like a sleigh. It took several hours. When I arrived I called a number of men together. They helped me build a fire, clean and spit the boar and set it above the fire to gently roast. We had a party that night; a great party and all our friends came and ate the beast which had killed my wife. Justice had been done.

Chapter 7

Early one Sunday morning a few weeks after Mary's death, a message arrived from the Laird inviting me to join him for Sunday luncheon at the Manor House. A rare honour. I washed and dressed carefully, made arrangements for John's care and made my way to the Manor House at the appointed time.

The Laird welcomed me warmly and offered me a glass of porter which we drank as we sat in his study. I sat there trying hard to concentrate as I gazed enviously at the row upon row of books on his shelves. I told him that I was intent on bettering myself and expanding my knowledge and asked if it might be possible to borrow the odd tome from his collection. To my joy, he was effusive and would be delighted for me to do so, asking only that I let his housekeeper, Grace, know when I came and went.

He asked how I was coping without Mary. The true answer was 'badly', but I told him I was trying to come to terms with the changed situation.

He changed the subject and told me there were a number of things he wanted to talk to me about. The first was that a decent period had now passed since the death of MacTavish. He wished to confirm my appointment as Head Gamekeeper if I was willing to accept the role. I said that I would be delighted to and he went on to outline various details of the appointment. He reminded me that I would now have responsibility for the three additional assistant gamekeepers on the adjoining estate and should pick up that responsibility as a matter of urgency as MacTavish had not been able to manage it properly for some time. I asked him how it was that we were responsible for activities on that estate. There is an old country tradition that, when things have happened on the wrong side of the blanket, they are not discussed. Everyone knows about them, but they are never spoken of. I had the distinct impression that this might have been one of those situations. Everyone else knew all the delicious details, I did not.

I pressed the matter as I did not see how I could reasonably manage the estate in total ignorance of the history whilst everyone else was fully conversant with the facts. He told me that the adjoining estate was known as 'The Chase'. The Laird of 'The Chase' had been betrothed to my Laird's mother and had drawn up a marriage settlement under which the entire estate became the property of my Laird's mother in the event of the Chase Laird's death. The marriage was solemnised and, five days later, the Chase Laird was killed in a hunting accident. Later my Laird's mother married his father and the entire Chase estate came into the ownership of our Manor Estate. Well, now I knew although, somewhat enigmatically, he added that, as a young boy, he recalled that there had been rumours of a sudden and unexplained disappearance of some of the previous Laird's family, following his riding accident. However, he knew nothing further of the matter.

He moved on to speak of MacTavish's house. It had now been fully restored and he considered it a more fitting residence for my new status. I was happy to accept the point, not least because our cottage still seemed to have Mary's ghost at times and the change would help to exorcise that. I was to move in at my earliest convenience.

His third point surprised me; it was regarding John. He said he had been watching John's progress since I had been appointed overseer. John was clearly a bright lad and he thought that, with appropriate schooling, he could go much further. He told me that at John's current age he had been sent away to boarding school. His father had endowed a bursary at that school to pay for the schooling of bright pupils unable to fund the cost of their education. He had written to the school to enquire if the bursary could be made available for John and had received their agreement. He asked what I thought about the idea.

The idea was a complete bolt from the blue and I had to think about it carefully. Without doubt, John was a bright boy and would probably flourish with some good tuition but, with his mother only recently dead, how would he react? I had already started to realise that ensuring that John was properly fed and catered for whilst I was out of the house for hours on end was becoming a problem. On the other hand, he was increasingly good company and I would miss him. In the end I thanked the Laird for the proposal and left the matter open saying that I would ask John for his reaction to the offer.

Business over, we moved through to the dining room where an excellent meal was served. The Laird was a lively conversationalist and kept up a stream of banter and conversation throughout the meal. We talked about many aspects of work on the Estate and, as on previous occasions, he asked my opinion on a range of subjects. It was a delightful repast and I was grateful to the Laird for his caring attention of my state.

The following day I took John into the forest for a long walk. I told him of the Laird's offer and proposal and helped him weigh the pros and cons. However, it was quickly apparent that he was attracted by the idea of some challenging tuition amongst boys of his own age. Touchingly, he was solicitous of how I would manage without him but I encouraged him to take the opportunity if he really wanted it.

At the end of our walk and discussion I sent word to the Laird that we would like to accept the offer. I recruited two of our neighbours to make new clothes for John to take, including some that were too large as he was going through a fast-growing stage. I had one of them sew a number of sovereigns into the hem of his vestment so that he would not be penniless and, on the appointed day I walked with him to the town from whence the Post Chaise would convey him to his destination. I am not certain which one of us was more emotional but it was tough to part. He may have been sired by another but, beyond doubt, he was my son and the son of my recently deceased wife. I walked slowly home feeling that all I had achieved was for nothing; the two people in the world I most cared about were gone from me.

Over the next few days I vacated my cottage and moved my possessions into what I still regarded as MacTavish's house – but now it was mine. After the fire, only the shell had remained and so everything within the house was now new and pristine. It was huge with umpteen rooms and was, by my weak standards, very posh. It was also very, very lonely. It had stabling for three horses and I resolved to acquire a horse and learn to ride it, to help me in my work. On my next visit to town I acquired such a beast, a very tame beast called Neddy. It would never win any race but it did convey me slowly but safely around the Estate.

I threw myself into my work and filled every hour in a futile attempt to forget. It did not work. Wherever I went and whatever I did, the image of Mary or of John would appear in my mind and mock my feeble efforts to escape them. Eventually, letters started to arrive from John. They were full of news of a world I could not understand but I knew at least that he was alive, that he was happy and fulfilled. Something in my life had gone right.

The Laird had reminded me that I was now responsible for three assistant gamekeepers on the adjoining estate. I now knew a little of the history of the arrangement but did know that I needed to meet the incumbent assistant gamekeepers and take control of the situation. I studied the map on the wall of MacTavish's office, saddled up Neddy and set forth for new lands to meet my new charges.

Thinking back, it must have been at least two or three years since MacTavish was in a fit state to call on them. They were sorry to hear of his demise but all three assistant gamekeepers were studiously unimpressed with the young upstart (me) who appeared in his stead. I was not fazed. By now I knew the role of a gamekeeper backwards and had the authority of my appointment. One look at the results of their stewardship showed me their shortcomings and I quickly reduced them to quivering wrecks, fearful for their livelihood.

From here, I progressively rebuilt their confidence, explained what I needed from them and arranged a series of shoots on their parts of the estate for the following season. I carefully checked that they clearly understood my requirements and would work to achieve them.

Before leaving the estate, I visited the old hall. The family had long since died out and it was in the care of an elderly housekeeper and her maid. It had been some time since I had eaten and I asked for refreshment. The housekeeper was rather surly but the refreshments finally arrived, care of the maid. She was a beautiful lass, slim and petite and with a long, slender neck. She was exquisite and had a face and smile to die for; her smile seemed to light up the room. I guessed that she was probably in her mid-twenties. I tried to engage her in conversation but, by signs, she explained to me that she was mute, dumb. Although there was obviously a problem with her vocal chords, there was nothing wrong with her ears and she could clearly hear everything I said to her. Despite her lack of speech, I felt a wonderful warmth and lightness of spirit in her presence. I ate the refreshments and thanked her then sought out the housekeeper and asked the maid's name. It was Caitlin. I rode home with the image of Caitlin's smile imprinted on my memory.

On my return I made occasion to report to the Laird on my visit and the arrangements I had made to host some of the following year's shoots on that estate. I omitted to mention Caitlin. I had a huge programme of work ahead of me and settled down to catch up with the requirements.

With John away, my new house seemed vast and daunting. Oft time I would awake in the middle of the night and wander through its many rooms; why? I know not. But instinctively I was not at ease. It occurred to me that it might be a good plan to employ a housekeeper and my mind went instantly to the memory of Caitlin's lovely smile and I resolved to visit her again. In the meantime I threw myself into my work with a new obsession and a will to ensure that everything was perfect.

In my spare time I took up the Laird's kind offer and started to visit his study when he was out. The knowledge those bookshelves contained was breath-taking. There were volumes on animal husbandry and plant husbandry; there were vast treatise on physical, metaphysical and philosophical subjects; there were translations of classical works such as Homer and Virgil. In short, it was a cornucopia of accumulated knowledge to satiate my desire for learning. I chose as my first study a volume on estate management from which I knew I could learn much. I burnt many a candle as I read, long into the nights and soon returned to the source for more.

The postal system was in its infancy in those days and not well developed but I did periodically receive letters from John. It was clear that he was happy. The learning was challenging but he was keeping abreast. He had made lots of new friends and, although he missed me and our Estate, he was emphatic that it had been a good move.

A month later found me back on the road to The Chase ostensibly to visit my charges but really to see Caitlin again. I called at the house first and told the housekeeper that I intended to stay the night and asked her to prepare a room for me. I then went off to call again on each of the assistant gamekeepers. My reception was better on this occasion. They had clearly recognised that I was definitely their new boss and were anxious to impress upon me that they had absorbed my instructions and were preparing for the planned shoots. They had obviously conferred since my last visit and were of one accord.

At the end of the day I returned to the hall. A fire was blazing in the hearth in the reception room, there was a drink at my elbow, the meal was ready for whenever it suited me and my room was prepared for later. Best of all, Caitlin was at hand to cater to my every request. Since my last visit I had wondered several times if I had been correct in my assessment of her, or had my memory simply exaggerated her loveliness and the warmth of her smile. But no, she was beautiful, breathtakingly beautiful; the sort of inner-warmth that finds a path to the heart and, with it, she was attentive to my every need. I recalled something that I had read recently from the Laird's library about Helen of Troy. Like her, Caitlin's smile could have 'launched a thousand ships and burnt the topless towers of Ilium'.

At the end of the evening I called her and the housekeeper to the reception room. I told them that I was looking for a housekeeper for my own home and asked whether Caitlin would be interested. They were both surprised. I suggested that they consider the matter overnight and give me an answer in the morning, if they were ready.

The following morning they served me an excellent breakfast. Whilst I was eating it Caitlin came and stood before me. She looked me in the eye and nodded vigorously. "Does that mean that you are interested in coming to be my housekeeper?" I asked and she nodded vigorously again.
"Right," I continued. "I will clear the matter with the Laird and, if he is in agreement, I will come to collect you in a few weeks' time."

I left shortly after breakfast and, on my return to the Estate, sought the Laird's permission. He was puzzled why I should want a mute as housekeeper, but he had not seen her. A fortnight later I rode out to The Chase again and returned to my house with her.

I gave Caitlin a lovely bedroom and allowed her to settle in. I told her that my comings and goings were often erratic and unpredictable. What I needed was for her to maintain the house in good order, have meals available for me when I did show and to act in all respects as a good housekeeper. I need not have worried; she turned out to be a treasure.

I was painfully aware that I was probably ten or more years older than she. That did little to supress my carnal desires, and each time I looked at her I wanted to sweep her up into my arms. Instead, I kept myself in check and behaved with propriety. In return, the house sparkled from top to toe; meals appeared as if by magic within minutes of my arrival and the visage of her beautiful, smiling face was constantly before me. She made and mended my clothes and seemed almost to sense requirements before they were uttered. All this, and perfect peace.

Mind you, she may have been mute, but she was brilliant in her communication. With seemingly little effort she was always able to communicate her thoughts to me. Her face was hugely expressive and her hands were always able to reinforce her facial expressions to explain her meaning.

John was due home from school for the summer recess and I knew this might be a difficult test for my new domestic arrangement. I journeyed into town to meet him and prepare him for the shock of another woman in the house, potentially displacing his mother. The first shock, however, was mine. In the few short months he had been away he seemed to have grown six inches. More changed though was his demeanour. He was confident and worldly. He knew who he was and was proud of it. I was stunned by the change which had come over him.

On our journey home I told him that I had engaged a housekeeper to keep the house in order, I explained that she was mute and that he would need to make allowances for her. He seemed understanding but, when we entered the house and he looked at her, he went totally silent and simply gazed at her. I noticed a bulge appear at the front of his pants and realised that he was as spell-bound as I had been. I had competition. That summer he followed her around like a pet spaniel.

I took John out with me on most days that summer. It was partly to give Caitlin a break but also to give him an understanding of my work. From our discussions about his schooling I had already realised that it was unlikely he would want to follow in my footsteps but I felt it would be useful for him to have some measure to gauge his future by. We grew closer together that summer than we had ever been and he enjoyed the physical nature of my job. I missed him when he finally returned to start his next year at the school.

Chapter 8

We were deep into the shooting season again and I was up and out at day-break each morning and never returned until after dark. I had no complaints and Caitlin was invariably there to greet me with her lovely smile. Truth to tell, I did fancy her enormously and found it hard to keep my lust under control at times. However, I succeeded and was unerringly kind and gentle towards her. She seemed to blossom in my service and I perceived a happiness in her demeanour which gave an even greater lustre to her beautiful smile. Nothing was too great a trouble for her and all was done in care of me.

The shoots were good that year. Since my elevation to Head Gamekeeper, I had set new and higher standards and requirements for my woodsmen and assistant gamekeepers. I tried to avoid being the sort of ogre that MacTavish had initially seemed, but I left my assistants in no doubt of my expectations for them. Conditions on the ground were perfect, the quantity of game was almost embarrassingly profuse and between us we had weeded out some of the unrulier elements amongst the beaters and dogs.

Our clients were ecstatic about the shoots that season and were invariably generous with both their praise and their purses.

The end of January brought the season to a close and I had more time to devote to other activities. On market day I resolved to visit the town as we were running low on various supplies. I decided to take Caitlin with me and it was quickly obvious that she had never been to town before. As a mute, she had been mewed up in The Chase since birth and had seen and heard little beyond its walls until she came to be my housekeeper. She stood in the market enthralled at the sights and sounds and at the sheer number of people. Then she started running from stall to stall to see what treasures each held. She took my hand and pulled me across to several stalls to show me what delights she had found. Her face was so expressive and so full of the joy and enchantment of the moment and of her new experiences that I felt the magic of her excitement.

One of the stalls had bolts of fabric and I picked one up and draped it around her. She shook her head and pointed to another so I did likewise with that. She had chosen well and looked lovely so I purchased the material for her to make clothes for herself. All morning we crossed from one stall to the next and I was happy to spend some of my money on her; she glowed with happiness. In the middle of the day I took her into the inn and ordered luncheon for us both. Like all else that day, it was new to her and her happiness was obvious. At the end of the day we loaded Neddy with our purchases and made our way back home; Caitlin radiating happiness all the while.

The Laird received a request from an eminent gentleman to be taken deer-stalking and he came over to discuss it with me. I had plenty of experience of stalking, but there was an old retainer on the Estate who was even better. He gloried in the name of Yeoman Muckle. Yeoman had spent his career stalking deer with clients. He was incredibly ancient and it occurred to me that we could not expect him to continue stalking for many more seasons. But for the present, he regularly walked out on the hills and he knew still where the deer congregated. He had also identified one old stag which was infirm. He wanted it taken out so that younger contenders could take its place and ensure the strength of the herd.

Yeoman had us up and out two hours before daybreak and we walked to the feeding ground by the light of the moon. I had brought Neddy with me so that we could bear home our quarry, if we were successful. For the final half hour,

Yeoman insisted that we maintain silence and Neddy was tethered to a tree and left behind. We were down-wind of the herd so that they were less likely to detect our presence as our scent or the slightest sound would have spooked them and they would melt from the scene.

We came to a steep hill and Yeoman instructed us to climb it in single file, him leading the way. As we approached the summit he signalled for us to keep our heads below the skyline and we crawled forward, seeking a place to go to ground. We found such a place and lay on our stomachs and were, at last, allowed to peep over the summit of the hill. The scene was breath-taking. Below us was a rich pasture with seventy or eighty deer grazing contentedly in the early dawn light.

Yeoman whispered that our quarry was not there. We lay there for perhaps twenty minutes, watching the tranquil scene as the sky gradually lightened. Finally, there was a movement in one corner of the pasture and several more deer entered, led by a huge stag with magnificent antlers. He was our quarry but he was limping slightly and I understood why Yeoman had picked him out to be culled. We waited patiently whilst he and his harem of hinds settled down to eat at which point Yeoman signalled our guest to ready his long-range riffle; he did likewise with his. I held my breath for an age as our guest waited for the ideal moment. Suddenly there was a loud report beside me but the shot missed. A split second later Yeoman's riffle exploded and the stag fell to the ground. Within moments there was not another deer in sight.

Yeoman and our guest rose and advanced to claim their prize. I headed back from whence we had come to collect Neddy so that we could bear the trophy home. When I caught up with the pair they had already released the intestines and were standing over the stag admiring the enormous beast. It was magnificent. Yeoman was pointing to an old scar, generously trying to convince our guest that he had winged it, thus allowing Yeoman to bring it down. I was not certain whether our guest was convinced. I most certainly was not.

I covered Neddy's head with a sack to avoid scaring him whilst we lifted our quarry onto his back. When all was ready I removed the sack and we headed for home where the Laird entertained us to a magnificent breakfast. Whether he believed he had hit the stag or not, our guest had enjoyed the morning and resolved to visit again next year.

I had the rest of the day free and took the opportunity to visit my old home and my river. Jason was not around but I took the time to sit on my old bench and to watch the river. It was peaceful and, as always, cleansing. I sat there remembering past times. I thought of Mary and how the river had brought her to me. I thought of John and looked forward to his return for the summer. I thought of my father and all that he had taught me and how the thoroughness of his tuition had enabled me to gain the exalted heights of Head Gamekeeper which I now enjoyed. I thought of my mother, but the memory was so dim that it was difficult to conjure up her face in my memory.

Jason had still not appeared by mid-afternoon so I rose and commenced my homeward journey. I wanted to inspect a particular area of land so ignored the bridle path and struck-off across country. I heard the sound of an axe biting into wood and came across Caleb who, by now, was a competent woodsman. We had a long chat and he told me of the work programme he had agreed with Jason. It was clear that they were working well together. At length I bade him farewell and continued on my way.

I was about halfway back to my home, passing through some heavy undergrowth when I accidentally stood on the tail of an adder. Before I could react, the creature whipped round and I felt its fangs bite deep into my leg before it slithered off to hide. I took out my knife and made a deep incision in my leg where it had been bitten, to try to bleed out the poison before it entered my bloodstream. I paused briefly to consider whether I should try to return to Caleb but decided to continue my way home. It seemed to take forever and I thought I could already feel a numbness in my veins.

I called for Caitlin as I entered the house and told her what had happened. I flopped down in a chair and she poured water from the kettle on the range and proceeded to bathe my wound. I was feeling decidedly faint and finally lost consciousness.

I knew little of the days that followed. I drifted in and out of consciousness aware only of Caitlin's presence. At one point I was aware that she had somehow managed to carry me to the bed and had stripped and washed me. In another brief lucid period I was aware that she was feeding me a loose gruel. I could taste herbs in it and wondered if it was some form or woodland medicine. On another occasion I heard voices and realised that she had ushered the Laird into the room. He was shaking his head and she shooed him away as I drifted back into sleep.

I learned later that I had lain there for nearly two weeks. I awoke on one occasion towards the end of that period to find Caitlin's face very close to mine, examining my face with obvious concern. Devoid of inhibitions, I reached up and pulled her face to mine and kissed her long and passionately. I sensed that she appeared to respond when, thankfully, I passed out again and thus avoided facing the embarrassment of my action.

At last I was able to rise from my bed and move about the house although, for several more days I spent most of my time in a chair. Caitlin was now on a mission to feed me to help restore my strength and she prepared some delightful meals to tempt my appetite. One night we sat around the fire together after dinner. I was starting to feel much recovered and I spent several minutes complimenting her and thanking her for all her kind ministrations in restoring me to health. I was happy and was smiling broadly at her. She responded with her lovely smile and then made a strange gesture. She touched her lips and then pointed to my lips.

It seemed that she had perhaps enjoyed her initiation into kissing but I pretended not to understand the gesture and said "show me what you mean". She came across and knelt beside my chair and again touched her lips, then touched mine and then hers again. I knew perfectly well what she meant but feigned ignorance to ensure that she would be the one to initiate any action. Again I said I was not sure what she meant and asked her to show me. She put her arms around my neck and pulled my face down towards hers. She kissed me, gently at first and then with increasing passion and urgency. Her lips were as soft and gentle as the morning dew; her arms and embrace as hot and fiery as a summer's day. It was clear that the whole business was new to her, but she learnt quickly. Within minutes, our kisses became more fervent and intense. I looked into her eyes and saw that they radiated joy and pure love. Our hands started to explore each other and liked both what they found and the feeling it imparted. I was totally lost in the beauty of this lovely young woman and my entire body responded to the joy of those heavenly kisses. Would that the moment should last for ever.

At length, the fire guttered in the hearth as a log burnt through and fell. We rose and Caitlin took my hand and led me through to my bedroom. Silently she undressed me, neatly folding my clothes as she progressed. Then she signalled that I should help to undress her. I did this slowly and sensuously, pausing at each point to kiss her again. When we were both naked I held her away at arm's-length so that I could look at her properly; she was slim and lithe and incredibly lovely. But I could tell that she was shy and embarrassed so I folded her into my arms and felt the thrill of her body next to mine. We stood there for a few moments, before retiring into the bed.

I had always enjoyed the times I had shared in bed with Mary, but Catlin was different. Caitlin had been starved of affection all her life and she was hungry for love. Her body was warm and soft, it felt gorgeous to touch and to hold. I ran my hands over her body and she responded to my every move, rising to meet my touch. She was insatiable and I was totally exhausted when I finally fell asleep in her arms.

Chapter 9

As the new day dawned I was forced to conclude that, if I was strong enough for what had taken place the previous evening, I must be fit enough to return to work. I rose and dressed, then kissed those lovely lips again and left her in our warm bed. It was growing light outside and I made my way to the Manor House to report to the Laird. He was surprised to see me and told me he thought he was going to have to find another Head Gamekeeper.

We talked at length and he relayed everything that had happened whilst I had been unconscious. Everything appeared to be under control but he was anxious to point out that Matthew Jamison was in his busiest period and was desperately in need of assistance. I bade the Laird farewell and went straightway to seek out Matthew and place myself at his disposal.

I found Matthew in his office struggling with mountains of paperwork and asked how I could help. He pushed the entire pile of papers across the desk towards me.
"Here," he said, "You're good at paperwork. Take this pile off me and sort it then let me know what I need to know.
"Fine!" I said as he retreated out the door, and I settled down to work. I hated sedentary, clerical work as much as Matthew did but rationalised that it was probably a sensible way of getting back into work, still weakened by my recent illness. By the end of the afternoon I had everything sorted, properly scheduled and listed and a summary ready for Matthew's action.

At the end of that first day I made my way back to my house. No sooner had I entered and closed the door behind me that I was besieged by Caitlin. She kissed me as though we had been parted for a year and she did it with such tenderness and love that I adored every moment of it. Finally, she paused for breath and led me to the table. She had prepared my favourite meal as a way of rebuilding my health and strength and I consumed it with relish. At the end of the meal I stayed idly seated whilst she cleared up. As she finished I rose to put another log on the fire. She took the wood from my hand and returned it to the basket. Then she took my hand and led me through into the bedroom. She had obviously been thinking about the previous night whilst I had been out and she was excited, very excited. The whole business was new to her but she had some new ideas and wanted to experiment. I clearly had a lot to learn. That was a wonderful summer. As with Mary, it never occurred to us to formally get married and in any event, there was no clergyman for many a mile to 'church' us. We simply went on living together. That was the normal way of things and no one thought evil of it.

As my strength returned, I flung myself back into my work and spent much of the next few weeks helping Matthew to organise and run his fishing events.

In due time John came to spend the summer holidays with us. I was concerned that he might think my relationship with Caitlin too early, too brash. Fortunately, he quickly accepted the arrangement and confided in me that he was pleased I had found a soul-mate and that I would not be alone in my 'old age'. I found it interesting to see oneself through one's children's eyes. John joined me on most days that summer and he was increasingly competent around the Estate. Initially he helped 'nanny' the fishermen, removed the flies caught in the rear of their pants and held the keep-nets to land their catches. As the summer progressed he helped me to organise the forthcoming shoots and was there to join in the feverish excitement of the 'Glorious Twelfth'. Had he a mind to it, I would happily have trained him up to be an assistant Gamekeeper. He shyly showed me his report card from school. It was outstanding and he was way ahead of his compatriots in every subject. He had already set his heart on going on to university and planned to study law. As always, I hated his departure but his was a different world from mine and I knew I could not understand it.

Shoots were planned for each area on The Chase early this season. I told Caitlin and asked whether she would like to join me for a visit to her old home. Her reaction amazed me. A look of terror came across her face and she backed away from me into a corner, violently shaking her head and mouthing the words "No, no, no!"
I had no idea what evils the memory of The Chase held for her but she made it very clear that she would not be returning. I calmed her down and made her understand that I accepted her refusal and would not pursue the matter. Her relief was tangible and within minutes I found myself naked again and back in bed as she showed her gratitude. I made certain never again to mention the subject of The Chase to her.

Our nightly activities continued unabated and I freely confess the joy I experienced in Caitlin's presence and in her body. She was unstinting and it came as no surprise when she announced a couple of months later that she was pregnant. She had been feeling strange for a week or two but, in her innocence, had no idea what the problem was. She had shared her symptoms with one of the other wives who immediately recognised the cause and gave her the good news. My love for Caitlin was so great that I delighted in the news and looked forward to the new arrival.

I made a quick visit to The Chase estate to check on their readiness for the coming season. There was less game than I would have liked to have seen but, in most respects, the assistant gamekeepers were ready. Between the three of them they had recruited an army or beaters and ensured that the ground was suitable for the guns.

I called at The Chase house and checked that the housekeeper fully understood what was required for the luncheons and at what hour; also that she had arranged transport for the victuals. I could not help wondering what horrors had taken place there which had so spooked Caitlin's memory. In the event we had three good shoots on The Chase. Afterwards I sought out the assistant gamekeepers and the housekeeper and thanked them and shared the rewards with them all.

The season continued and we had many excellent shoots that year. All the same, there was a corporate sigh of relief when the season ended and we had time to recover and get on top of other work. It was also the time when we started to round up the remaining game and gather eggs to breed the next generation.

Our baby was due in March and Caitlin and I eagerly looked forward to the event. I was very careful never to refer to the baby daughter Mary and I had lost. We were full of hope and I was confident that this time, all would be well. Caitlin's tiny body grew enormous as though it would burst, but she bore it with fortitude and patience. For my part, it was almost a relief not to be called upon to fulfil Caitlin's latest fantasy each night. Almost!

As the time for the arrival came close, I recruited two of the local mothers to help Caitlin through her labour and to deliver the baby. I had been there once before and had no wish to experience the process again. When the waters broke and the contractions started I called for the mothers to attend. I then went to find Yeoman Muckle and asked if he was going out stalking that evening. He said he had not planned to but it was a fine moon-lit night and sounded like a perfect opportunity.

We set off for the hills and the feeding ground. I had no intention of shooting anything but the adventure occupied my mind fully and kept it off happenings back at home. We reached the feeding ground shortly after midnight and had the privilege of gazing down on a huge herd of deer grazing peacefully in the meadow under the light of the moon. I lay there, spell-bound.

Yeoman suddenly stiffened. His keen eye had spotted another lame stag. He asked if our visitor from last year would be visiting again this year. If he was, that stag was the perfect target. We lay there watching for about an hour until we suddenly realised that we were both getting chilled and we rose and retraced our steps. At his cottage door I thanked Yeoman and made my way back to my house. As I approached, I heard a baby cry. The door opened and one of the ladies called out "You've got a son." I asked if I could come in to see him and was told "No, not yet."

A few minutes later she leaned out of the door again and called "And a daughter".

I was the proud father of twins and a few minutes after that I was invited in to meet my new children. They were beautiful but poor Caitlin looked decidedly shattered. I asked one of the ladies if she knew of a wet nurse who might be able to help Caitlin care for the bairns. By good luck, she did know of someone who lived nearer the town. At my request she promised to travel over as soon as it was light to see if she could help.

The wet nurse duly arrived late morning and immediately took charge of the twins. Caitlin was relieved as she was exhausted from the birth and needed to rest. I installed the nurse in one of the spare bedrooms and she took the twins in there with her to have them always close at hand. I had already made a cradle whilst waiting for the baby's arrival and I now quickly fabricated a second for the twin. The nurse took excellent care of the bairns and attended to their every need.

Caitlin recovered a couple of days later and was up and about, helping the nurse wherever she could. By signs, she asked me what we should call the babies. I said I would like to name the boy after my father, the same name as mine, Richard. Caitlin was happy with that. I went on to say that I would like to name the lass after the woman I loved most in all the world, Caitlin. Caitlin looked embarrassed but then nodded shyly, accepting the idea. So, there we were, we had welcomed Richard and Caitlin into our family. At an early opportunity I wrote to John at boarding school and told him of the new additions to the family. By return, he wrote a lovely letter congratulating us both and saying how much he was looking forward to meeting the new arrivals.

It was now some fifteen years since John had arrived on my doorstep and I had quite forgotten how babies organise one's life and household. But they were gorgeous creatures.

Chapter 10

The forests on our Estate were ancient, comprising a wide variety of broad-leaf deciduous trees and large areas of coniferous woods with various pines and firs. Some were known to have been laid-down by monarchs in the early middle-ages to create hunting grounds for their entertainment. Other parts were believed to have been laid-down by nature over many millennia.

When I had been a woodsman, tutored by me father, I had ensured that there were wide fire-breaks in the areas of pine forest to arrest the flames should fire break out. In travelling round in my current role, I had become aware that the fire-breaks in some parts of the forest were narrow or non-existent. I mentioned my concern to the Laird during one of our conversations. He thanked me and promised to raise it with the Head Forester.

I believe he did, but nothing substantial changed and the inevitable happened. That summer was long and hot and it did not rain for weeks on end. An area of dry grass caught fire in the heat and, in no time, there was a major forest fire. Everyone on the Estate turned out to fight the fire but there was no handy supply of water and our only weapon was besom brooms which we used to beat down the flames. We fought the fire in shifts for three or four days but the fire would not be controlled. It continued to burn until it reached the natural break of the lake which bordered the estate and had nowhere else to go. Even then one or other of us stood guard for several more days to ensure that there was no new outbreak and there was considerable relief when there was a heavy storm to quench any lingering sparks. Fortunately, the lost woodland was in an area where we did not normally host shoots otherwise there would have been a serious loss of income for the estate.

We had lost many hundreds of acres of prime forest and the Laird was not amused. He summoned the Head Forester and summarily dismissed him on the spot for failing to carry out the instruction to increase fire breaks.

A few days later I received an invitation from the Laird to call on him. So far as I was concerned, that was equivalent to a royal command and I wasted no time in answering his summons. I entered his study and found him in a highly agitated state, pacing up and down the room.

"Richard," he said. "I need your help." He went on to tell me that he had recently become engaged to a famous beauty and the marriage was to take place in a month's time. The local rumour machine had been active lately and I was already aware of this.

"The wedding will, of course, be in the bride's parish and I shall leave for there in three weeks' time. It is our intention that we will depart straight after the wedding and travel throughout Europe, possibly even further afield. I do not expect that we will return for at least six months, probably longer. Until now, I have always acted as the Estate Manager. I cannot do that whilst I am away and, when I return, I do not intend to take up that role again."

My immediate thought was how the Estate would be managed in his absence but, without prompting, he went on to address that matter. He told me that he was angry with himself over the matter of the forest firebreaks and the subsequent loss of a huge area of valuable forest. He should have noticed the danger without waiting for me to raise it and, having been alerted by me and having instructed the Head Forester, he should have ensured that the work was completed urgently. He blamed himself.

"Richard, you have proved yourself a skilful, honest and reliable servant over a number of years. You have fulfilled every task I have given you and you have done so thoroughly and with humility and compassion. You have a thorough knowledge and care for the Estate. I want you to take over as Estate Manager."

It would be a serious understatement for me to say that I was surprised, but he continued.

"Until my return, I would like you and your family to move into the Manor House and to act as my person in all matters to do with the Estate. All my staff are your staff in my absence and I shall expect them to obey your every instruction. All personnel, including senior personnel such as Matthew Jamison, will be responsible to you. I have chosen you for the task because I believe that you are the best man for the job and that you will do it with diligence and compassion." He went on to tell me what my remuneration would be for the role and asked if I thought that adequate. To me it sounded like riches beyond the realms of avarice and I happily agreed. However, I pointed out that I would need to make some changes to ensure that there were no gaps in the chain of command.

At this point the Laird called for his housekeeper, Grace, and his treasurer, Gregory, to join us. He relayed the same message to them making it abundantly clear that I was in all respects his person, during his absence and was to be honoured and treated as such. He told Grace that I and my family would be moving into the house and would entertain honoured guests here in his absence. He also asked Grace to help me organise a wedding feast in the Great Barn for everyone on the Estate, to celebrate his marriage.

He told Gregory that his treasury was at my disposal and any requests were to be regarded as though from himself, the Laird. He noted that it was probable that I would need to do some reorganisation and that funding might be required for this.

As an afterthought he told us that the eminent Lord who we had taken stalking last year had asked to visit again, just after the Laird was due to depart. He instructed Grace to ensure that he was feasted lavishly and that I would be his host.

Grace and Gregory left us and we covered some other items of business before I left. Back in my house I collapsed into a chair and stared at the wall. How on earth was I going to tackle this task? There were over one hundred people on the Estate and suddenly, I was responsible for them all. Caitlin joined me and showed alarm at the look on my face. I relayed the conversation of the morning and told her that, for the next six months at least, she was to become the lady of the manor.

This change in my fortunes was frightening and I was not sure that I was ready for it or equipped to undertake the task. I had risen from the humblest beginnings and had little social sophistication, yet I was being called upon to manage a huge estate and entertain men of rank and fortune. I needed to think. I took myself off to my childhood cottage and sat on the bench to watch my river and listen to its song. Like my life, it was flowing fast, far too fast. I wanted the river to wash away all my fears, pressures and concerns, to carry them far away and leave me cleansed, refreshed and free. Instead, my thoughts got caught in the eddies at the side of the river and simply went around and around. Its babbling song held no balm, no offer to help me shoulder this heavy responsibility. I was on my own.

Since his dismissal, I was short of a Head Forester and, following my promotion, a Head Gamekeeper. Should I simply try to replace them, or did I need to consider some reorganisation of the various roles? At this point I had no clear answer so I watched the river and let it wash over all my concerns.

Jason returned late in the afternoon. He brought two mugs of cordial from the cottage and came to join me on the bench. I had already established a regard for Jason's knowledge and ability in both game keeping and in forestry. I wanted to speak with him about the relationship between Assistant Gamekeepers and woodsmen. Until now, each had reported to a different head but, in reality, they worked fairly closely together. What was his experience? Jason told me that at his previous estate, the woodsman had reported to the assistant gamekeeper and the two worked as a team, thus confirming my thoughts. He went on to share other thoughts about the organisation at his previous employment, all of which helped to clarify my thinking. Without committing myself I also made very tentative enquiries on how he would like to see his career progress. He had no great ambitions but we both knew that he was capable of greater challenges, if called upon. I thanked him and made my way home, sticking to the bridle paths on this occasion.

Before reaching home I called in on Yeoman Muckle and warned him of the forthcoming visit of the eminent Lord and asked for his assistance to lead the stalking. Yeoman rather caustically expressed the hope that his Lordship's aim had improved since last year.

The next morning I sought out Matthew Jamison. I was fairly clear in my mind that the skills of fishing and maintaining the rivers were quite different from those of game keeping and forestry management but I wanted to know if he had any thoughts on possible changes. The Laird had already told Matthew of my elevation and he was generous in his congratulations and support. In truth, he would not have wanted the job. I explained that I saw fishing and game keeping as very separate activities but that I was considering how to reorganise for the future to simplify the task of managing the Estate, and wondered if he had any thoughts or plans. We talked around the subject for a couple of hours. I shared his view that the river gillies were rarely stretched, but it was not easy to see how to extend their roles. The only thought he had was that it could be helpful to develop a central hatchery for spawning fry so that they could be released back into each section of the river. It would take several years before the young fry finally returned to the river to lay their eggs, but it seemed like a worthwhile long-term project. I said that, provided it could be done with existing personnel numbers, I would be happy to endorse it and asked Matthew to let me have an assessment of the cost.

I spent time with the Laird before he departed and told him my thoughts for the future. He made it very clear before we started the conversation that it was my decision and my judgement, but he was happy to chat the matter over, if I thought he could add to the discussion. I first told him of my discussion with Matthew and that I had endorsed his idea for a central hatchery. By then I had Matthew's assessment of the cost and it was extremely modest.

I moved on and told him that I did not propose to replace the Head Forester. I intended to promote Jason to Overseer and to instruct that assistant gamekeepers would in future be responsible for the woodsman on their territory. Together they would organise the forestry work, the hatchlings and the shoots; the assistant gamekeepers would report to Jason who would in turn, report to me. I also intended to appoint one of the three gamekeepers on The Chase as the working overseer for that estate and would require him to report to me each month.

I had not yet had an opportunity to consider the other trades such as the farm workers or farrier, but would look into that shortly. The Laird accepted my plans and then added some thoughts and advice on the farmers and other trades.

The Laird departed on the appointed day and I moved my family into the Manor House. Apart from the two cradles, we did not need to take any furniture with us as the house was fully furnished. Grace welcomed us and I was relieved that she was immediately taken with the twins. Had she been less than enthusiastic, our stay might have been more problematic.

Caitlin was ecstatic at her new surroundings and ran around the house excitedly exploring each room. The wet nurse had come with us and Grace had organised a room for her which would also act as a nursery.

Chapter 11

I sent a message to Jason asking him to come over for a discussion. Whilst I waited, I went out to find Matthew. I located him in his office and told him to go ahead with his idea for a central hatchery for fish fry, reiterating that it should be done within his existing manning levels. Although I did not mention it, I liked the idea and wondered whether the same principle might be applied to hatching chicks. Incubating eggs required the cooperation of a large number of broody hens for weeks on end and later, a little heat for a month or more whilst the chicks developed. Different solutions were applied in different parts of the estate, with differing results. It might be possible to devise a more controllable solution if applied centrally.

Jason arrived later and I took him into the study in the Manor House. He was aware of my new, elevated status and I explained that I had been thinking about our recent conversation and wanted to make some changes to the way things were organised on the Estate. There would be no replacement for the Head Forester and, as we had discussed, each assistant gamekeeper would be responsible for the woodsman in his part of the forest. The two of them would work together to control both the woodland and the game in their part of the Estate.

I went on to tell him that I did not intend to replace myself as Head Gamekeeper. I was looking for an overseer to take charge of all the teams and organise the shoots and asked if he would be interested in the role. He confirmed that he was interested but asked what plans I had for his existing patch? I had no immediate solution but we would work together to find one.

Jason was to take possession of the cottage near the Estate office that Mary and I had occupied when I was first appointed overseer. He was to have the use of the office adjoining my house, the one which had originally been MacTavish's. Finally, I talked to him about the forest fire which had resulted in the departure of the Head Forester. Jason was an experienced countryman. I impressed upon him that both he and I must be constantly on the alert for such issues. They could be of any nature but it was up to us to spot potential issues or dangers and to address them before they became problems.

When he had left, I asked Grace to join me in the study. We discussed arrangements for the party to celebrate the Laird's wedding. She clearly had the matter in hand, had organised the catering and had recruited an army of helpers. She told me the menu she had planned and it sounded excellent. We agreed the start time and arranged for messages to be sent out to every employee on the Estate, inviting them to the Great Barn.

We then went on to discuss arrangements for the eminent Lord who was due to arrive the following day for the stalking. He and I would have an early dinner in the evening before setting out with Yeoman. When we returned we would take a leisurely and substantial breakfast and she would have some champagne cooling in the hope that there was a success to celebrate.

I welcomed his Lordship warmly on his arrival. He was fully aware that the Laird would be absent but maintained that he would have soundly warned him against marrying which he considered a dangerous and over-rated pastime. We dined together and he was excellent company. Throughout the meal he regaled me with endless anecdotes of amusing incidents in the House of Lords or on his visits to other members of the landed gentry. It was most certainly not a dull meal.

After dinner we each retired to our beds to take a brief rest before our planned outing and I left instructions for us to be roused at two in the morning. It seemed that I had only just closed my eyes when the call came. I arose and dressed but found his Lordship already downstairs when I descended. The stalking was always planned for a night when there would be a moon and this was no exception. I called for Neddy to be brought round. There were plenty of horses in our stables and I planned to give Neddy to Jason for his use, but for tonight, he was the ideal beast of burden.

We made our way across to Yeoman's cottage and found him already waiting for us. He had been out the previous dawn to check on the location of the herd and we followed the same path and plan as the previous year, tethering the horse a good way from our destination. We reached the top of the hill and peered cautiously over the brow. There was not a deer to be seen. We lay there for a few minutes lest some might appear, but it was not to be.

After a little while Yeoman signalled us to rise and follow him. We retraced our steps down the hill and then circled round to the right. We crossed the pasture where we had expected the deer to be feeding and cautiously ascended a small hill at the far side. Once more we peered cautiously over the brow of that hill; fortunately, the entire herd was gathered below us in the early morning light. Yeoman examined the herd carefully and finally spotted the injured stag. He pointed it out to his Lordship and both made themselves comfortable and readied their riffles. It seemed to take him an age but finally his long-range riffle sang out. Yeoman was ready with his to follow-up, but he was not needed. His Lordship had aimed true this time.

I set off to retrieve Neddy to carry our trophy back to the Manor House and returned in time to hear his Lordship say "Yeoman, you are a rotten liar. I know perfectly well that I missed that blasted stag last year. But this, this is mine. Thank you."

We were a merry party as we made our way home. The three of us managed to consume several bottles of champagne and, after a hearty breakfast, retired back to our several beds to sleep off the effects. We met again for a light luncheon before his Lordship departed. He had enjoyed his visit and was still bubbling with excitement. A most successful visit.

I spent the rest of the day with Caitlin and the twins. They were already putting on weight and I realised that I would need to make them some cots 'ere too long, for they would soon have outgrown their cradles. The wet nurse was doing a good job of caring for them but I was also conscious that, because Caitlin was unable to speak, the only voice the twins heard was that of the nurse. I resolved that I too would talk to them at every opportunity.

I left early the following morning for The Chase in a pony and trap. I had studied the map on the wall of the office and noticed that there was a point where the boundaries between the two estates overlapped with a deep incursion of our Estate land into the geography of The Chase. It was labelled 'Staley Moor'. I had ruminated on this for some time, pondering whether it might afford some opportunity for rationalisation of activities between the two estates.

I had already decided in my mind which of the three assistant gamekeepers I would prefer to act as overseer for The Chase and I wanted to call on him first to see if he was interested. His name was Raphael. I found Raphael and talked to him about the appointment and what standards and procedures I would wish him to adopt. Obviously, it would enhance his wages and he was pleased to accept. The Chase mainly comprised grouse moors so the question of woodsmen did not apply. I discussed with him the question of the overlapping land areas at Staley Moor. He said that he had thought for years that it was a nonsense. Like the land on The Chase estate, it was largely grouse moors. He and his two colleagues could easily manage that area in addition to their existing work. That was wonderful news and meant that I could transfer the assistant gamekeeper from there to Jason's old patch. There might even be a spare woodsman; I would have to look at that.

I set off with Raphael to call on the other two assistant gamekeepers. They had heard about my preferment but it was important for them to understand that Raphael was now their boss and they would be expected to honour him as such. Both of them appeared to fully accept the situation and agreed to take their instructions from Raphael. For my part, I asked that he should attend the Estate office at the monthly pay meeting. He was to collect the pay for his colleagues and would report to me to update me on matters on The Chase, before leaving.

I was pleased with the day's work and, on my return called upon Jason and told him to transfer the assistant gamekeeper from Staley Moor to his old patch. I was still thinking about the additional woodsman and wanted to look at the various options.

The Laird's wedding was to take place on the coming Saturday and the Estate party in the Great Barn was set to commence at six o'clock that evening. I went through the plans again with Grace. She was extremely competent and everything was in hand. Caitlin and I were to act as hosts on the top table but very little else was required of us. I had already learned that there was to be some music and I checked with Caitlin that she was prepared to join with me, to start the dancing and we practiced a few tentative steps in the private of our bedroom, before setting out.

We arrived just a few minutes after six and the barn was already packed. We sat at the top table and Grace and her kitchen staff served the meal. It tasted superb and she had made certain that there was ample for second-helpings for anyone who wanted. I had organised several barrels of mead and cider and everyone was merry by the time the sweet was served. At the end of the meal I stood and proposed a toast "to the Laird, our benefactor and protector, and to his lovely bride; long life and happiness". Everyone in the barn stood and echoed the toast and, as they sat down, the music struck-up.

I took Caitlin's hand and we danced around the barn to much applause. No one else joined in so, after an appropriate time, I whispered to her to grab hold of Matthew and continue the dance. I apprehended Grace and whirled her around several times before moving on to one of the wives. Fortunately, by then, many others had joined the fray. Caitlin and I returned to our seats and held hands under the table and the dance went on.

Still holding her hand, we circulated round the tables. By now, I knew most people on the Estate but I also took the opportunity to introduce myself to any I did not recognise. Caitlin was unable to join in the conversations but her smile slew the heart of every man we addressed. She was, as always, breathtakingly beautiful. At about nine o'clock I checked that there was still ample beverage in the barrels and we quietly left the barn so that all could relax and be themselves. It had been a successful evening and I knew that even Caitlin had enjoyed it. I asked her so as we retired to bed. Her hands slipped below the covers in response and silently did unmentionable and rather exciting things. She was incorrigible.

<u>Chapter 12</u>

I had a few priorities for the coming week. I wanted to visit the farming community, I wanted to go through the event programme with Jason, and I wanted to talk with the woodsman from Staley Moor. I chose to do them in reverse order.

I caught up with the woodsman in the forest near Staley Moor, his name was Jack. He already knew that his assistant gamekeeper had been transferred elsewhere in the Estate. I talked to him about the transfer of Staley Moor to marry up with activities on The Chase estate. He agreed that it made sense. He was only really operating on the fringe of the forest which adjoined it. I talked with him at length to discover his abilities and knowledge. I wanted to assure him that there would still be a job for him but I had not yet decided where. I had an initial experiment I wanted him to assist me with. It was the development of a trial egg hatchery to see if we could improve the success rate of hatching chicks. He would report to Jason as the overseer but he and I would develop the project to see if it could succeed.

In addition, I asked if he would do some private work for me in his spare time, build two children's cots for my twins. I made it very clear that this had to be done in his own private time and I would pay him privately for his work. I had already realised that I did not have the time to do it.

I brought him to the Estate office so that we could talk with Jason. To be certain there was no misunderstanding, I told Jason that I had commissioned Jack to make some cots for me in his spare time and that I would be paying him privately for that work. We then went on to talk about the hatchery. It transpired that Jason had been involved in a similar project on his previous estate before it was broken up. He had some knowledge of the plans and together we drew up a sketch of a hatchery unit to try out the concept. I asked Jack to construct such a unit and run a test in it.

It was finished within a week. We collected a selection of eggs, lit the carefully designed heating unit and waited to see the results. We met each day and monitored the heat and humidity in the unit. Initially there was a danger that we would cook the eggs, then that they might become too cold. Finally, we worked out how to keep the temperature at the optimum level and maintain the right level of humidity. At the end of the incubation period, over half the eggs had hatched. We kept the new chicks in the warmth of the incubator whilst they developed and later shipped them out to the new assistant gamekeeper on Jason's old patch and asked him to monitor their progress.

In the meantime, Jack produced two excellent children's cots in his spare time and I paid him for them, as agreed.

We modified the design of the hatchery to improve the controllability of the heating and introduced a second and larger batch of eggs. The fire had to be monitored at regular intervals but, maintaining a more constant temperature, we increased the success rate to over sixty percent. Bearing in mind that we had no idea how old some of the eggs were, I felt that this was a pretty acceptable result. We agreed to extend the trial to one location in the forest and settled upon Jason's old patch.

The incubation period for a pheasant's egg is between three and four weeks. Jack enlarged the hatchery and we arranged that all eggs from that region would be brought to the hatchery at weekly intervals. Without doubt, it was an outstanding success. The only reservation was one of size or capacity. At the end of the trial period we had achieved nearly seventy percent success in the hatchings. The process was clearly successful, but capacity was an issue.

We had produced less than two thousand chicks over the period. We probably needed ten times that number.

We continued to monitor the success of the unit whilst seeking ways to develop it commercially. At the end of the breeding season we had produced six thousand chicks. An excellent result but still insufficient to supply the estate as a whole. I left the problem in Jack's hands to consider the next stage.

I also had a secondary activity for him. Big strides had been made in introducing or increasing the fire breaks in the pine forests since the fire. However, there were a number of areas where I was not satisfied that the gap would prevent a fire leaping from one side to the other should we experience similar conditions. I gave Jack a roving commission to increase the safety gap in a number of areas throughout the Estate. I was not going to risk a repeat of the horrors of the previous year. Unlike the former Head Forester, I also made regular inspections of the progress at the selected spots.

Whilst all this was going on, I spent time with Jason going through the event programme for the Estate in detail. There were a large number of fixtures and each had to be carefully planned. Jason needed to decide on which part of the Estate each would take place, check that the conditions were right and the game plentiful, ensure that beaters had been engaged and organise accommodation, transport and refreshments. A fair task. Over the next few months Jason and I would go through that list again and again and again.

In the meantime, I needed to learn about farming. The farms on the Estate were all located in the lowlands towards the southern end of the Estate. There were a dozen small farms and I visited them all over the next few days. Each farm included both dairy herds and arable land where a variety of crops were grown. There was no attempt at specialisation and the farms were poor and of low grade. Until his death the previous autumn there had been an ancient farmer who was ostensibly the overall farms manager.

The previous autumn I had had a long conversation about farming with one of our guests at the shoot. He had told me that there was a major revolution taking place in farming in the south of England. There were new machines for sowing and reaping crops, there were new crop-rotation methods which were increasing yields, there were new, more productive breeds of cattle. On my return to the Manor House I immediately wrote to him. I reminded him of our conversation and said that I wanted to identify someone who was familiar with these changes to come and act as overall manager for the farms and introduce the new machines and farming methods.

He replied promptly and told me that he had a very capable young man who did know all the latest developments. His name was Andrew Green. Andrew was chaffing at the bit because there were several older managers on the estate who were equally knowledgeable and he wanted an opportunity to spread his wings. This sounded ideal and I wrote back inviting Andrew to visit our Estate. Two weeks later he turned up at the Manor House and I spent several hours talking with him, quickly realising that he was knowledgeable on his subject. Our only problem was that we were from opposite ends of the country; I from this isolated corner of the Lake District with a strong Cumberland accent, Andrew from the home-counties, speaking in what I later came to realise was a very posh voice. It took a while before we were able to fully understand each other's accent but I liked him immediately and we got on well together.

Andrew and I travelled back down to the farms and inspected each in turn. As we went around, I introduced him to the farmers as their new manager. I could read their reactions in their faces. Who was this boy? How can he possibly teach me anything about farming? And, by the way, what language was he speaking? I had already discussed with Andrew the probability of resistance from entrenched farmers. From our discussions I was confident that he would find a way to overcome the problem and gain their trust. However, I warned him to try to take his charges with him, rather than imposing changes on them.

I installed Andrew in the former farm manager's house and I agreed a budget with him on how much he could spend on machinery and new blood strains. Before leaving, I arranged that he would come and report to me after his first month.

On my return to the Manor, I found that John had arrived home for his summer vacation. He was much enamoured with the Manor House and declared that it was a more fitting residence for his aged father. He also fell immediately in love with the twins. They were still very tiny and not yet sitting up but they were already developing characters of their own and were a joy to behold. John spent long hours with them, cooing and gurgling in response to their little noises. John told me proudly that he was not returning to school at the end of the holidays. He had been awarded a place at university and would be starting on his planned law course this autumn.

As in previous years, I took John with me on my various visits round the Estate and he enjoyed the change after all the months of studying. We called in on Matthew Jamison and he showed us the fish hatchery he was developing. He had sited it in a spot where there was a flow of fresh water to constantly renew the water in his tanks. The tanks were teeming with life. There was a progression of holding tanks with tiny creatures in the first graduating to good size fry in the last. He was justifiably proud of the experiment and explained that the latter were ready to be returned to the river.

John and I caught up with Jack, the spare woodsman. He had made an impressive improvement in almost all of the designated fire breaks and I was pleased. He had logged the cut timber and I asked him to arrange to have it hauled to the Manor House in time for winter. I made a mental note to ask Jason to identify the next project for Jack when he had finished the last of the fire-breaks.

We rode out each day in the pony and trap. We visited each of the assistant gamekeepers and woodsmen throughout the Estate. Without exception, the teams appeared to be working well together. I carefully noted the quantity of game at each location and the ground conditions for the shoots. All was ready.

I was due to visit The Chase estate and took John with me. We met up with each of our men there. Raphael, the overseer, was clearly in charge and on top of his work. I had him ride out with us to the Staley Moor area which had formerly been operated as part of the Manor House Estate but he had now taken under his wing. It was in perfect condition and I complimented him on the progress. I told him that we would stage the Glorious Twelfth opening shoot there and he was pleased.

A few days later, Andrew Green came to report on his first month as farm Manager. He was clearly happy and enjoying himself. He had found no difficulty in convincing his charges that he knew every bit as much as they did about farming and he was already starting to introduce some new ideas and methods. He had purchased a new bull and a boar to improve the blood-lines in the cattle and the pigs. He planned to do the same with the sheep later in the year. He had found that the condition of the soil was poor and he intended to sow several fields with turnips and mangelwurzels as a winter feed-stuff for the cattle. These had also been shown to improve soil quality.

With the time for sowing winter wheat drawing near, he had ordered one of the new horse-drawn seed drills which sowed the seed more economically in neat rows. This brought him on to the subject of the size of the fields. With the present tiny farm units, many of the fields were also tiny. The seed drill would enable a farmer to sow much increased areas but it would only really make sense if the size of the fields was increased. He wanted to amalgamate several of the small farms and enlarge the size of the fields. He had brought with him a sketch of the farms and his proposed changes.

We both knew that there was likely to be resistance to such a plan and we talked through the people on the various farms. On two of the farms most affected, the farmers were ageing and had no family to follow them. We decided that we would ask these farmers to help with the work of changing the layout and enlarging the fields, following which they would be offered retirement cottages on the Estate, and a pension. The only other farmer who would be significantly affected would end up in charge of a larger farm which would probably increase his income.

I asked Andrew if he wished me to visit and pronounce the changes. He declined. It was his problem and, with the proposed arrangements we had discussed, he was happy to tackle it.

The shooting season was upon us and, as on the previous year, I took John with me on the Glorious Twelfth. Our guests had a superb day's sport and Raphael and his assistants did us proud. We dined back at the Manor House that evening and paid our respects to the first grouse downed, as we ate it. The organisation and the sport had been first-rate and Jason had done a good job managing the programme from the centre.

The season continued but I took a couple of days out to visit the farms. I took John with me as he had not been there before. We met up with Andrew Green and he gave us a conducted tour of the entire area. The transformation which had taken place in the short period since his arrival, was amazing. The farms all looked neat and business-like. Hedges had been grubbed-up and the fields enlarged and there were already winter crops peering through the ground in the fields. We saw the magnificent bull and the new boar Andrew had purchased. Several of the cows and sows had already been serviced and the farmers were looking forward to some healthy arrivals. I spoke to the two farmers who were to be retired off. They were very happy with the arrangement, as was the farmer who now had a larger farm. All seemed to be going well and Andrew spent some time outlining his further ideas and plans. In particular, he wanted to introduce greater specialisation on individual farms, rather than continuing the current generalisation.

I asked him if the cottages were ready for the retiring farmers. At the moment, he only had one available. The other was occupied by a young girl whose parents had both died in recent months. He did not have the heart to throw her out. I asked to see the lass, her name was Morag and she was twelve years old. Morag was a confident young lady and talked to us at length. Following the death of her parents, she had no other family and nowhere to go.

I told Morag about the twins. They would shortly be weaned and the wet nurse would leave. Because Caitlin was unable to speak to them, they would rarely hear a human voice. I asked Morag if she would like to come to the Manor House and take care of them. The idea appealed to her immediately. She spent half an hour collecting her meagre possessions and then joined John and myself in the pony trap for the journey home. John was much nearer her in age and the two chatted ceaselessly on the journey.

On our arrival I introduced her to Caitlin whose approbation was essential. We then introduced her to the twins and she fell immediately in love with them. She picked each of them up in turn and talked to them and tickled them. They chuckled their responses to her and I felt that this was going to be a good arrangement.

<u>Chapter 13</u>

I received a letter from the Laird. He and his bride planned to travel further and they would not be returning for several more months. A pity in a way as I would gladly have surrendered all responsibilities to him and gone to sit beside my river. Then I recalled that he did not intend to resume his former involvement in the running of the Estate on his return. There was no way out. All the problems were my problems.

Our experiments with hatching chicks played on my mind. I made a point of finding Jack to see if he had made any progress. I was pleased to find that he had continued to develop the idea. In a very remote part of the forest he had built a hideously long hut which he had heavily insulated with thatch. He had installed a stone-built, slow-burning hearth in the centre which could be fed from outside, without even entering the hut and he had inveigled the blacksmith into making him some ducting which channelled the heat throughout the contraption and also heated a water tank to maintain the humidity level. Inside he had erected endless shelving to hold thousands of eggs and there was plenty of space for newly hatched chicks to keep warm for a month until they were hardy enough to be shipped out. He was ready to try the contraption and he certainly had my support. The only draw-back was that, like a charcoal burner, it needed someone to watch the heating day and night. However, he declared himself willing to do this for the next couple of months to see what results we could achieve.

Through Jason, I organised for each of the assistant gamekeepers to visit the site on a weekly basis. For the first three weeks they would bring their eggs. Jack would place the eggs on the shelves and rotate them at regular intervals. When the eggs had hatched and the chicks had hardened for a few weeks, the gamekeepers would hopefully return home with young chicks which they would then place in their own feeding enclosures. The experiment worked well. We had to make some adjustments over time but the hatch success and the volumes of chicks hatched convinced me that this was a worthwhile exercise.

Whilst this was progressing, the Saturday for the Harvest supper arrived. I spoke with Grace about her plans and it was clear that, as always, she was fully on top of the arrangements. Caitlin and I acted as hosts and I made the traditional speech on behalf of the Laird, but with less skill and humour than he would have brought to the task. My main contribution was to make absolutely certain that there was sufficient drink for everyone. Once again, Caitlin and I started the dancing and it was good to feel that we were by now very much accepted. It was a really enjoyable evening.

The shoots recommenced the following week and, with the exception of the break for Christmas, they continued right through to the end of January. As always, there was a communal sigh of relief when the season ended and we had time to start our winter duties.

I spent some time with Caitlin and the twins and Morag. The wet nurse had left and Morag was now in sole charge of the nursery. It had been the making of her and she had blossomed since her arrival. It was difficult to know whether she adored the children most or if it was them that adored her. It did not matter; the arrangement was working well. The twins were nearly one year old. Both were crawling all over the place and Richard was very close to walking. They were not yet saying real words but they made some lovely sounds, encouraged by Morag. Caitlin was happy with the arrangement too and relied heavily on Morag.

I took time out to visit Andrew Green down at the farms. He had clearly stamped his authority on his farm workers and they were working well together. The improvements since my first visit were obvious and it was good to see that Andrew was enjoying himself. So far as he was concerned he was his own boss and did not get interference from others. The winter crops had been harvested and consumed and early spring planting was already in place. There were some fine, strong new cattle and pigs in the fields and there was a clear air of industry and productivity across the farms. Andrew had ordered some further machinery to mechanise harvesting and the whole place had a buzz about it. I congratulated him on the progress he had made and listened to his next set of plans. Everything was under control.

When I returned to the Manor House I found a note from Raphael saying that the housekeeper at The Chase had been found dead. She had apparently fallen down stairs and there was no one else in the house to help her.

The Chase was an anachronism and I wanted to know more about the place. Initially when I asked Caitlin, she was unwilling to help but I pressed her for answers.
Was there anyone else who used the house? No!
Did guests stay there at the shoots? No!
How long was it since it had been properly used? Caitlin held up all he fingers; ten years.
I was going to have to think what to do about the place.

By the following post I received a letter from the Laird. It had been in the post for several weeks and said that they expected to arrive back at the end of March. Today was the second of April.

I roused Grace and we quickly reviewed what was necessary. I would evacuate my family today, back to the house I had occupied as Head Gamekeeper. She would organise maids to clean the house urgently, light the fires and make up the master bedroom. Food would be organised with cold food for a late-night arrival or quickly readied main repast for a daytime arrival.

I assembled a number of the men to transport cots, toys and our personal effects back to our old home whilst furious activity took place in the Manor House. By tea time, all was ready. In the event, they did not arrive back for a further three days. By then, calm had been restored. The servants lined up outside the front of the Manor House to welcome the return of the Laird and his wife.

We had not previously met the bride, Elizabeth. She was a very beautiful lady but, whereas I had started from the bottom rung of the social ladder, she had started from the top – and stayed there. Although she went out of her way to be friendly, I felt rather out of my class. The Laird looked fit, well and happy and it was good to see him returned.

I was summoned to the Manor House on the second day after their return. He told me that Gregory had reported that the finances were in good order and that the year had been successful with an increase in revenues and some reduction in outgoings. I spent a long time telling him how things were on the Estate. He did not appear to be particularly interested or attentive, but rather distracted. At length he reminded me that he did not intend to get involved again with running the Estate. If there were specific issues or questions, he was willing to respond. Otherwise it was in my hands and I should continue as before.

I told him that there was one item on which I did need his input. The housekeeper at The Chase had died a few days ago and the house was empty. What would he like me to do there? He said that he and Elizabeth would ride out there sometime and we would have another discussion after they returned.

I was summoned again a few days later. Apparently, Elizabeth was not particularly enamoured with the Manor House which she considered far too large for her future requirements. However, she had fallen instantly in love with

The Chase. They had decided to have it refurbished and redecorated. They would then staff it for their needs and they would live there. I was to return to the Manor House and host our shooting and fishing guests there. Caitlin was thrilled that we were to return to the Manor House; a dream come true. My only fear was that the Laird might want to take Grace to The Chase with him. I did not relish the thought of having to find a replacement to match her competency.

Work on The Chase was put in hand as a matter of urgency. Elizabeth and the Laird had clearly decided that they would prefer to be away from the Manor House and avoid involvement in the entertaining which had traditionally been part of the fishing and shooting parties. The numbers involved in the fishing were usually fewer than for the shoots and they tolerated them through the early summer. However, they were anxious to depart before the larger numbers arrived in the autumn. I found this quite surprising. Elizabeth was obviously a snob but shunned the opportunity to rub shoulders with some of the most influential people in the land. Their plan was to relocate before the arrival of the party for the Glorious Twelfth. A tight schedule.

An army of workmen were recruited to work on The Chase and the refurbishment continued throughout the summer. No expense was spared and on a brief visit I saw that the house was to be sumptuous in every respect. On one of my increasingly brief meetings with the Laird I asked him if he was intending to take any of the staff from the Manor House to his new home, as I would need to recruit replacements in time for the shooting season. To my immense relief he told me that Elizabeth intended to bring her entire staff from her old home and he did not expect to need anyone from the Estate. I thanked the stars in heaven.

Despite their urging, The Chase was nowhere near complete by the beginning of August. The two of them decamped back to Elizabeth's old home to wait until they could move into The Chase. In a manner, it was a relief and the pace of life at the Manor House calmed with their departure.

I took time out to return to my childhood home near to the island in the bend of the river. Jason's replacement assistant gamekeeper was nowhere to be seen and I trespassed back to the bench outside the cottage and spent several hours watching the flow of the river and listening to its song.

I needed to think. Things had changed; the Laird had effectively abdicated his responsibility for and his involvement in the running of the Estate. It was no longer his Estate, it was mine. Yes, he still owned the land and would continue to live off the income of the Estate, but from here on, every decision, every idea, every change was mine. What did I want?

If I did nothing, nothing would happen. If I made a mistake, it would be my mistake. If I achieved a success, it would be my success, in part at least. What did I want? There was no one to advise me, no friendly hand to guide me. I was alone and alone responsible for the success or failure of the Estate. Like the days of my years, the water in the river would continue to flow; it would not stop running and no single drop of water would ever pass that way again. I needed to grab the moment, drink the water of the river before it passed by. This time I felt encouragement in the song of my siren maiden from the depths; she quieted my mind, slowed my thoughts and made me think through the problems which lay ahead.

Before I left the river, I had compiled in my head a list of actions for the coming months. The first, and possibly the most important, was to talk to our clients and to see what they wanted.

Chapter 14

As always, the guest-list and the arrangements for the Glorious Twelfth had been finalised many months before the day. There is always high excitement from both guests and hosts for the first event of the season. Meticulous care had been applied to planning every aspect of the visit by all the workers on the Estate. The guests arrived already excited for the day ahead and determined to enjoy themselves. It was the same every year.

It was an auspicious company that assembled that evening. It included a learned professor, two bishops and several members of the House of Lords. A sumptuous dinner had been arranged for our guests on their arrival and we ate and drank all the evening.

For the first time I felt that this was truly my party. I had organised it, I was the host, I would lead them out to the shoot and, to all intents and purposes, I was the Laird of the manor. Coming from a lowly background I had not learned airs and graces from childhood. But I had observed carefully, I had learned and I was not concerned that our guests would look down on me or belittle me. It was almost to the contrary; most of my guests had known me as Overseer and then Head Gamekeeper and they respected my knowledge and experience.

The conversation ran freely with some wonderful tales from all sides of the table. Whenever I could, I steered it towards learning about other shoots and their practices; part of my determination to learn from our customers. My first two discoveries were that our shoots were the very best in this part of the country and, surprisingly, they were also the lowest cost for miles around. I was very happy that we should be the best, but not that we should simultaneously be the cheapest. Gregory was responsible for the finances and for sending out invitations and I quickly relayed this information to him so that he could make the necessary adjustments for future shoots.

I continued to probe on what they liked about our shooting parties. They were unanimous that the festive boards were excellent as was the catering on the shoots and I later congratulated Grace. They felt that the guest-rooms at the Manor House were a little tired and there were some mild complaints about the long distances they had to walk to the shoots. I took note of both of these comments. I resolved that we would refurbish the rooms and I would organise a conveyance which would deliver them in comfort to the birds.

Despite our bleary state, we were up early the following morning and on the grouse moor shortly after daybreak. It was a beautiful dawn and the morning's sport was first-rate. As tradition demanded, the first grouse downed was sent to the Manor House to be prepared for our dinner. One of our guests broke the Estate record for the largest ever bag for the first morning and was thrilled when I later presented him with a prize. We paused for the excellent luncheon which had been sent up from the Manor House but, whilst we ate, it started to rain heavily and persistently. There was a little more, rather half-hearted shooting but the party quickly lost heart and we tramped back to base, rather damp. During the afternoon we warmed ourselves before blazing fires and primed the inner-man with spirits so that we were all ready for the celebration meal later that evening. Obviously, there was disappointment that the day's sport had been curtailed prematurely but the morning had been so excellent that no one was inclined to complain. The following morning a leisurely breakfast was served and guests appeared as they were able and most left before the middle of the day.

Later that day I mentioned the 'tired rooms' comment to Grace. I asked her to have a critical look at each guest room and prepare a schedule of suggested improvements for us to discuss. Apart from any obviously urgent needs, most work would need to wait until the end of the season.

I then sought out Jason and congratulated him on the success of the first shoot. On some sheets of paper I sketched out the concept for a horse-drawn wagon to convey our guests to the shoots. It should have fixed rows of forward facings seats, steps at the rear and a structure to bear a canvass cover when it rained: one of the guests had described it as an horse-drawn omnibus. I wanted it made quickly so that we could use it throughout the season. I also wanted Jason to instruct and manage the construction of more hides for the shoots and simple covered open-sided barns at each main location where guests could take their lunches or shelter during storms. It took a little time for all this work to be completed but, by the time of the Harvest supper, they were in regular use.

The reputation of our shoots was spreading by word of mouth and more and more guests were asking to be included each year. That was a particularly wet autumn and returning guests clearly appreciated the improved facilities. Despite the rains, we had some excellent shoots and I saw it as my responsibility to ensure that our guests fully enjoyed their visit, whatever the weather, particularly as I intended to increase prices for the following season.

The Harvest Supper was its usual great celebration particularly as Andrew Green had brought a huge contingent from the farms and they were buzzing with the success they were achieving in improving yields from every source. It reminded me that I needed to make another visit to the farms. Caitlin and I started the dancing and once again, I felt very much the Laird of the Manor.

Shoots restarted straight after Harvest and, fortunately, the weather improved. Towards the middle of December, I rode across to The Chase. I had heard that the work was nearing completion and that the Laird and Elizabeth were planning to move in before Christmas. The Laird was visiting to inspect progress and I asked him whether he wished to return to the Manor House to host the traditional Christmas festivities and the dinner. He did not. Before leaving, I sought out the clerk of works. I told him that, when he laid-off his workmen he should send any reliable ones across to the Manor Estate with a note from himself. A plan was forming in my mind and I was confident that I could find work for them.

We held the traditional Christmas festivities. With Grace's assistance, presents had been secured for every child and whilst they were handed out, their parents received a generous noggin of mulled wine or spirits. We processed together down to the Great Barn for our Christmas Luncheon. By now the twins were about twenty-one months and were able to join in the festivities. They were highly mobile and I felt sorry for Morag as she had never a moments peace, chasing them around. However, it was clear that she adored the little scallywags, and they her.

For a long time, I had been aware that we were not caring fully for our stock of houses and cottages on the Estate. They were ageing and were not receiving attention. At the end of December, workmen started arriving from The Chase, where they had completed their allotted tasks. I intended to use them to refurbish the bedrooms in the Manor House once the guests had departed but, for the moment, I set them to work to progressively refurbish some of the Estate cottages, much to the delight of the occupants.

As always, the shoots continued through to the end of January and I continued my mission to learn from our guests. I wanted to learn how to increase their enjoyment of our shoots and I also wanted wider learning on developments in farming, fishing, forestry management and shoots. The improvements Andrew Green had introduced on our farms had whet my appetite. I wanted more and all sorts of ideas and useful information emerged in my various discussions.

I had already agreed with Grace the schedule of work which was necessary to bring the Manor House guest rooms up to an acceptable standard. As soon as the last guests had departed I moved the workmen into the Manor House, at the same time assuring our tenants that they would be returning to refurbish more cottages as soon as they had completed work on the Manor House. As well as the complete refurbishment of the rooms and furniture, Grace's proposals included the renewal of carpets, curtains and bed linen. Together we inspected each room as it was completed to ensure that we would be proud to have our guests lodged there. We were both pleased with the improvements which significantly raised the standard of the guest accommodation.

As the workmen finished their work in the bedrooms, they returned to refurbishing the cottages. I wanted my people to live in decent accommodation and that guided the level of work required.

I journeyed down to the farms to talk with Andrew Green. There were daily journeys and deliveries of milk, butter, cheese and eggs from the farms to the centre of the Estate. As I travelled I became aware for the first time how ridiculously circuitous and arduous the journey was. I resolved that we would create a direct bridleway between the two which would halve the journey. That was a project for Jack.

I allowed Andrew to regale me at length with the enormous increases in productivity that had been achieved, listened to his next set of rather revolutionary plans which his farm-hands had already signed on to and then cavilled at his next request for funding for the work. Finally I said to him "Very well, go ahead. Now, I want you to tell me what else I don't know that I don't know."

That puzzled him slightly until I explained that his ideas for the farms had been a revelation to me and I needed to get to know what else was happening in the world that could improve our Estate. That stumped him and he had to think for a while but finally came up with a few thoughts.

The first was that the old windmill was dying on its feet. It rarely operated satisfactorily and, when it did, was struggling to keep up with the increased volume of grain that they were producing. He proposed that we dig a mill-race and convert the mill to operate by waterwheel. That was hardly revolutionary technology but made good sense and, as we were now producing more grain than we needed on the estate, we would be able to sell the excess flour elsewhere. I told him to do it.

He next observed that the Estate did not sell much timber. I told him that this was partly because of the problems of transportation and also sawing facilities. I mentioned that on my journey down I had already resolved to improve the road which ran down to the farms and thence through to the rest of the world, but I did not have a solution for the sawing requirement. Andrew told me that, just like the proposed corn mill, most saw-mills now operated by water power. I realised that this could represent a new line of revenue for the Estate although I may need to reintroduce a forestry manager. As we discussed the idea it became obvious that both facilities would rarely be operating at the same time. They could, therefore be sited on the same stretch of river and share the same mill-building. I asked him to organise the construction of a saw-mill as part of his reorganisation of the corn mill.

"Anything else?" I asked.

"Isn't that enough for now?" Andrew replied. "There is still a lot of new stuff going on in farming, but I am on top of that.

There is plenty happening in wool and cotton spinning and weaving; but I don't think that is where our future lies." Before leaving, I told Andrew of the work I was having done to bring cottages up to an acceptable standard. When they had completed their work in and around the Manor House I intended to send them down to him so they could work on improving cottages and farm building in his area.

I returned home and immediately sought out Jack. I told him that I wanted him to prospect a new, fast, direct route from the Manor to the farms, as straight as the land would allow. When he had decided the course, he should start cutting timber from the southern end before progressively working his way back towards the Manor. The reason for this was that Andrew was going to build a saw-mill near to the farms. Starting from where the mill was to be sited, the timber could be cut for transportation as the road progressed. If we had any spare labour, I would send it down to assist him. Jack probably thought it was a crackpot idea, but by now he trusted me.

I had not spent much time with Matthew Jamison recently and I felt it was time to talk about any plans he had for the fishing. I congratulated him on the success of the previous season and also on the fish hatchery and asked him what other ideas he had. Matthew was not a great thinker and he had no ideas. He told me that he had received a large number of applications for the forthcoming season. It was fully booked and he was now having to reject any further applications and turn people away. That triggered an alarm in my brain and I started to enquire further. It transpired that he only ever allocated stands on the best parts of the river. I enquired whether, particularly with parties attending for more than one day, would it be possible for each fisherman to have some time on the best parts of the river and some on the less productive reaches. After a long debate he reluctantly conceded that it was possible and could render the overall visit more challenging and interesting. I asked him to try to double the numbers and liaise with Grace about accommodation and meals.

Work on refurbishing the rooms at the Manor House was now complete and the workmen were back progressively working through all the cottages on the Estate smartening them up, repairing defects and generally making them more pleasantly habitable. I wanted a contented workforce.

I caught up with Jason and asked him to accompany me on a tour of the Estate. As we journeyed I told him that I had asked Jack to start to cut a new road through to the farms. It was probable that work would keep him occupied for a year at the very least. We visited every part of the Estate and talked with all our employees. There were no obvious gripes and I was pleased with the work that had been done on the hides and shelters. I felt that our guests would appreciate them. We talked about minor improvements here and there but there were no obvious major projects.

We rode over to The Chase and spoke with Raphael. All seemed to be in order there although we did discuss the need to burn-off a particular area of heather moorland which had grown old and straggly. I insisted that it could only be done when the wind was set away from The Chase house.

I spent time with Gregory to speak about finances and treasury issues. I had already agreed a plan with him about the muted 'low cost' of our shoots. He knew too about the works on hides and shelters and the ongoing refurbishment of the cottages. I added information about Andrew's plans on the watermill, the saw mill and his various farm projects. I told him that I had instructed Jack to start cutting a roadway through from the manor to the farms and I would probably add additional labour when it became available. In due time there would be timber for sale. I asked him to identify markets and manage the financial aspects. I told him that I had agreed with Matthew that he would try to increase the occupancy of the fishing parties and that too would require managing.

I thought that was probably everything and asked him how the finances were going. Gregory still saw himself as the Laird's man, even if he rarely saw the Laird. He was cautious but did acknowledge that, although I appeared to be increasing expenditure, income was still increasing faster.

The fishing season was due to start shortly and I would be expected to entertain our guests. First, I took a couple of days out to celebrate the twin's second birthday. Caitlin and Morag had organised a party. We were all invited, as were another couple of tiny children who had been hatched on the Estate. It was a lovely occasion. Games had been organised as had special children's' birthday food and there was lots of fun. The twins were not yet talking people talk, but they were very communicative between the two of them and seemed to have a language of their own. I duly crawled about the floor and did all the things which were required of me, thankful that neither our posh guests nor my employees could see me.

Chapter 15

The start of the fishing season galvanised the Estate from its winter torpor. Preparations had been going on in the background throughout the winter but the appearance of guests on the Estate brought out the best in everyone as we remembered that our livelihood depended on our visitors' enjoyment.

Since our conversation about allocating fishermen two different locations during their visit, Matthew had reluctantly increased the number of visitors and I was anxious to see how they were coping with the less-productive stands on the river that Matthew had been avoiding. There seemed to be plenty of fish throughout the length of the river, the rods were happy and it did not appear to be a problem. Matthew suggested that some of the earliest hatchings which had been reintroduced in the upper reaches of the river were possibly now returning for the first time. That sounded rather early, but whatever the reason, the success encouraged him and he progressively increased the numbers on each fishing event.

I joined most events for at least part of the day and entertained our guests royally each evening. I continued to listen to our visitors and to seek their ideas and opinions on how we might further enhance their experience at the Manor House. It was clear that they were appreciative of the improvements we had made to the bedrooms and facilities and I resolved that we would commission a similar upgrade to the general dining and reception areas, the following winter and spring. It was important that we maintain the Estate to a high standard and that our guests saw the Manor House as a desirable and enjoyable venue. If we were to increase our charges, the event had to been seen as value for money with standards to match our visitors' expectations.

When our guests left us, I wanted them to tell their friends about the magnificence of the Manor House Estate, as well as the unparalleled sport. I involved Grace in the discussions and asked her to start outlining some ideas for how we could make the place special. She agreed to do so but added a plea that she would like to see the kitchens and domestic facilities included in the refurbishment plan.

Since the final completion of work at The Chase, the clerk of works from there had joined his men working on our Estate. I was anxious to retain him and his labourers for the remainder of the year to complete the refurbishment of the Estate cottages before finally moving them back into the Manor House to upgrade the dining and reception areas. I spoke with him about the programme to ensure that he and his team would stay with us throughout. He was content. I also asked whether he would prefer his men to continue the cottage refurbishment work together or if he would be happy to split them and have half of them start on the cottages and buildings refurbishment down at the farm. He was happy to split them and I sent him off to Andrew Green with half his men to organise the work programme on the farm.

When John returned from university for his summer break that year he was no longer a boy; he was a grown man. He was tall and held his head high, proud of who he was. He was great company and I was happy to include him in many of the dinners for our guests, particularly when there were some younger visitors. He was fully able to hold his own in the conversations and had a fund of stories with which to regale the diners.

I had received word from Andrew that work on the flour mill was complete and the completion of the saw mill was imminent and I took John with me to inspect the work. As we neared the farms we came across Jack, hard at work on the new road. There was a long way still to go but he had made some very significant progress; I was delighted and thanked him. The trees he had cut down were stacked near to where the saw mill was sited, ready to be sawn.

We found Andrew talking to two men who I did not recognise. He broke-off to welcome me then explained that the two chaps had just arrived, looking for work. He had no current need of them, did I have any vacancies? They looked strong and fit so I talked to them briefly and then sent them off to join Jack in opening up the road. I made it clear that they were to follow Jack's instructions and I would expect them to work hard to earn their keep. When I saw Jack again later that day, he was clearly pleased to have some extra hands.

Andrew very proudly gave us a conducted tour of the new milling facility. A mill-race had been dug from some little way up river and a good force of water flowed through it. A water-wheel had been constructed on the side of the mill and was turning with the water from the race. Inside the mill the noise was horrendous but the grinding stones were flying round and flour was being ground and tumbling down a chute for collection. It was impressive.

Just then the miller threw a lever and work within that part of the building suddenly stopped. We were led through to another part of the building to see the almost complete saw mill. Over the saw-pit there was an enormous circular saw-blade with a diameter about as tall as a man. Andrew threw another lever and the huge blade started to revolve at speed, driven by the force of the same water wheel. I would have liked to have seen it operate but Andrew stopped the blade revolving and told us that he was not yet satisfied that it was properly balanced and ready for action. It was clear that if this mill operated successfully it would transform our ability to produce timber from the Estate.

Before we left we were treated to a guided tour of the farms and I was impressed with the continuing improvements. The enlarged fields were full of strong-looking crops and the pastures contained increasing herds of strong and healthy animals. Andrew had introduced specialisation to increase yields and the farm workers were proud of what they were achieving. So far as it is ever possible for a farm to be neat and tidy, they were.

I quickly checked with Andrew on the cottage refurbishment work. He had agreed a schedule of priorities with the clerk of works and work was progressing. He told me that the arrival of the builders had been another big boost to the morale of all those on that end of the Estate. They were increasingly proud, not only of what they were achieving, but also to be part of a progressive and caring Estate.

As the summer progressed I had a pony trap fitted out with seats for the twins and, on many Sunday afternoons we rode out as a family and often took a picnic. Caitlin would sit beside me on the driving seat and she loved the opportunity to see new parts of the estate. We often sat up there holding hands as we drove along. Morag would be behind us ensuring that all was well with the little ones. We found some wonderful places to stop and play and had some great fun. Mindful of Mary's demise, I always had my shotgun and ammunition handy, just in case. Thankfully, in all my years on the Estate I never encountered another wild boar.

These Sunday trips were useful for me in that they gave me opportunities to visit various parts of the Estate and keep an eye on activities. One Sunday we left earlier than usual and I drove the family all the way down to the farms. Apart from game, very few creatures were kept in the vicinity of the Manor House and I wanted to show the children a variety of livestock; cows, sheep, pigs, hens and so on. They were fascinated and spent the return journey amusing each other, trying to reproduce sounds such as the clucking of the hens. As always, Morag was with us and she was astounded at the changes which had taken place at the farms since her departure.

Whilst we were down there I took a sneaky look at Jack's new road and was pleased to see that, with the aid of his two assistants, he making excellent progress. It looked as though it might well be open by the end of the year. I also noted that, although many more trees had obviously been felled to make way for the road, the pile stacked up beside the new saw mill had not grown. The mill was obviously coping well with the volume.

Early in August our Sunday outing took us up to the Grouse moors so that I could be satisfied that all was ready. Realising that we were not too far from The Chase, Caitlin made it very clear that she did not want to go there. I had no particular wish to visit the house either. I had seen very little of the Laird since his return from his honeymoon and I was thoroughly enjoying the freedom his absence afforded. I no longer even bothered to let him know my plans or ideas. I just got on and did the things which I felt were right and for the long-term benefit of the Estate. The results were showing that they were the right things. Gregory was increasingly open with me and it was clear that, whilst we were investing heavily in the facilities and infrastructure, the Estate was becoming increasingly profitable.

The Glorious Twelfth was as glorious as ever. The usual distinguished company presented themselves and I entertained them royally. These were the visitors whom I had first started asking for ideas for improvements. They were tremendously impressed with the significant improvements in the bedroom accommodation and when I led them out the following morning to the new horse-drawn omnibus conveyance with seats to transport them to the moors, they knew that I had taken notice of their suggestions.

We had an excellent mornings sport with a good level of success. As I called time for luncheon it started to rain and I led the party to one of the new covered barns. I had had tables and chairs laid out in the barn and we were able eat our luncheon in comfort and in the dry. The storm passed and we eventually resumed the shoot but there were several pleasing comments about the innovation of the sheltered 'dining accommodation'.

It started to rain again towards the end of the afternoon and the guests were delighted to be able to ride back on the covered omnibus wagon, rather than traipsing wearily through the rain.

That evening we talked of the improvements we had made and planned for the Manor House and our visitors were very complimentary about the changes. One guest mentioned someone called Miss Tamsin Grey who had set herself up as an advisor on the refurbishment of stately homes. He had employed her to refurbish his house and had been delighted at the results. He recommended that I should contact her before beginning the next phase of the proposed work. I duly wrote to Miss Grey and invited her to visit the Estate.

Whilst I awaited a reply to the invitation, the shooting season got into full swing. The weather was reasonably fair that year and, with the additional facilities of the horse-drawn omnibus, new hides and the covered barns where guests could sit and take their luncheon in comfort, we had some most enjoyable shoots. I continued to ply guests with questions on how we could further improve their enjoyment and various little ideas continued to emerge.

Miss Tamsin Grey arrived shortly before Harvest. Grace joined our discussions and we spent time outlining some of the ideas we had. Tamsin was a strong-minded young woman who had clear ideas of her own on how things should be and we were quickly carried away in a whirlwind of possible improvements. Whilst I was striving for excellence, I needed to keep all our feet firmly on the ground. We devised a plan to use a goodly number of mirrors in the lounges and dining areas. This would give an increased impression of space and opulence and create an ambience which guests could enjoy. Tamsin had a good feel for furniture and soft furnishings and she and Grace soon had that side sown up.

We moved on to discuss the kitchens and ancillary areas. She had some excellent ideas on modern facilities and labour-saving devices and I could see that Grace was getting very enthusiastic. Miss Grey was far less than complimentary regarding the external surrounds of the Manor House which had received no attention over many years. It was untidy and haphazard and did nothing to enhance visitor's initial impression of the Manor. She championed the idea of a circular drive in front of the house with a statue in the centre and suggested that a portico would look impressive at the front with steps sweeping up to the front door. At the rear she recommended installing a large paved courtyard encircled by a low wall with benches where guests could sit to take their pre-prandial refreshments.

All the ideas sounded marvellous but a voice at the back of my mind was shouting "How much?" I asked her to prepare three estimates for the work; one for the dining and reception rooms, one for the kitchens and a third one for the external work. Tamsin took some measurements and made copious notes before departing.

The Saturday after her departure was the annual Harvest supper. Employees gathered from every corner of the Estate and we had a wonderful evening. It might have been wishful thinking but I thought I detected a particular joy in this year's gathering; all our people – my people - seemed to be happy and contented, there was a feeling that we were all working together and were a successful team. Caitlin and I took the twins, little Richard and Caitlin to the supper although we fed them first so that they would not have to wait forever. The twins were still not speaking properly but none-the-less went from table to table endearing themselves and inveigling treats from every quarter. When the dancing started, Caitlin and I took one twin each in our arms and the four of us danced round the room together, to the delight of the children. Then, whilst Morag entertained the children, the two of us visited every table and thanked everyone for their work that year.

When the quoted costs for the proposed work arrived from Tamsin Grey, they were eye-watering and I had to give some thought to how to approach the matter. The proposals were excellent and were precisely the sort of thing that was needed but there was no way I could slip the costs through unnoticed.

I liked the ideas for the proposed external work and thought about that first. The new road (already becoming referred to as 'Jack's highway') was nearing completion. It would start from the Manor House, head straight as a die through the countryside to the farms. It would pass through the farms and connect up with the turnpike road. It was the route that all our visitors would take in future, rather than the tortuous route they had followed in the past. The idea that it would sweep into a circular driveway in front of the Manor House at the north end was appealing, as was the thought of the statue in the centre and the portico with steps to the front door. The suggested paved courtyard at the rear of the house was an excellent idea. However, it was difficult to justify the cost outlined. I decided that we could almost certainly achieve most of that work internally using Estate labour and I would probably be able to hide the cost.

Having carefully inspected the kitchens and utility areas several times recently, I felt that work was necessary to enable our staff to continue to provide excellent feasts for our guests. I could see no way round that.

The proposed refurbishment costs for the dining and reception areas were incredibly high. I identified a number of discreet costs which could possibly be sacrificed and omitted from the schedule of work, but was rather loath to surrender them. I talked with Gregory who agreed that the costs would be rather hard to disguise and I decided that the best line of defence was attack. I arranged to ride across and talk with the Laird.

I had troubled him little on Estate issues for some time and I think that was in my favour. I started with an overview of how Estate income had risen over the past year and an estimate of how much I forecast it to rise further in the coming year. He liked that. I then launched into a diatribe of how our guests were demanding increasingly high standards in return for their increased entry fees. I told him that Lord THIS and Sir THAT had specifically recommended and requested improvements in various elements of our facilities. I got away with it. The Laird endorsed the proposed works and we were away. I wrote to Miss Tamsin Grey authorising the acquisition of the various effects and alerted my clerk of works that he and his labourers would be required from the first of February for the internal work and that, during any lull in that work, I wanted them to start the external landscaping.

The plan worked well. Mirrors and all the other requirements started to arrive throughout January and they started work under Tamsin's direction as soon as the last guests had departed. Jack's highway was completed just before Christmas and I moved Jack and his assistants to start to prepare the circular driveway as soon as they had finished the road. It was an extremely tight schedule to have the work completed before the opening of the fishing season and every other available person was drafted in to assist on the work and then on the paved courtyard area at the rear, as they became free. The front portico and steps awaited completion of the internal work but the entire project was completed by mid-April.

Grace was ecstatic about the improvements which had been made below stairs and I was invited down to view the results. It all looked very smart and business-like and the kitchen servants were proud to show me around the various new innovations. Gregory settled all the accounts which made rather a hole in the Estate finances. However, income was still increasing faster than expenditure and we were in profit before the end of the season.

I had occasion to visit some of the servants' quarters and rooms at the top of the building. I was not pleased. I suspected that they had received no attention since the house had been first built many years ago and they were not worthy of the standards we had set for the rest of the house, nor even for the refurbishment which had been completed on the Estate cottages. Before finally releasing the clerk of works and his team of labourers, I had them complete some simple redecoration and refurbishment of these rooms and replace broken beds and furniture. Compared with the rest of the work, it was a fairly low cost but worthwhile and necessary exercise and did much to improve the morale of the house-servants.

I asked Grace to review the carpets, curtains and bedding in those rooms to ensure they were acceptable and to replace any which were not. I also agreed with her that we would commission the making of identical smocks as a uniform for all the female staff and shirts in a similar material, plus a waistcoat for the men. The resulting attire gave a look of professionalism and pride to the team.

<u>Chapter 16</u>

The Manor House had always been an impressive building, but now it was absolutely stunning. It was transformed beyond recognition and I was delighted with the results. Visitors would leave the turnpike road and pass through the farms before joining 'Jack's Highway' which would take them, straight as a die up to the Manor. They would sweep through the impressive new gates into the circular court-yard, pass round the statue to halt in front of the portico where they would alight and their carriage would be taken from them round to the stables at the rear.

Our guests would then mount the steps of the portico between the mock-Corinthian pillars and pass into the marble hall. From there, they would be assailed by opulent furnishings and beautiful gilded mirrors on all sides, creating an impression of light and space. I felt that we had truly created something of excellence which fittingly enhanced the Manor House.

I took no part in discussions regarding the proposed sculpture to be positioned in the centre of the circular courtyard and left the matter entirely in the hands of Miss Grey. She had suggested that a fitting subject in keeping with activities on the Estate, would be Orion, the Hunter and had commissioned a famous London artist to do the work. I never met the man and he never met me. However, some on the Estate insinuated that the figure on the plinth bore a striking resemblance to myself. I made a point of never consulting a mirror, so was unable to comment.

Our early visitors arriving for the fishing season were truly impressed and delighted by the changes we had made. They admired the smart uniforms of the servants and several commented on how courteous and attentive the staff were. I am certain that the general ambience helped to increase the enjoyment and success of the early season.

For me, the great test would be the reaction of our traditional Glorious Twelfth visitors. If they liked it and had a successful and enjoyable visit then I would know that we had achieved our objective.

After the first party of visitors had left, there were two nights without guests. On the first evening we celebrated the twins' third birthday. By now they were seriously mobile and exceedingly vocal. Once again, we invited a couple of children of around their own age to join the party. Morag had organised a few simple games for them to play together although she declared that getting them all to do the same thing was rather like trying to herd cats. Each of them wandered off in a different direction in a tiny world of their own. We also quickly realised that no one was permitted to 'lose' in a game; there were just lots of different ways of winning and everyone received a little treat from the kitchens as a prize.

On the second evening I had decided to host a dinner for our senior staff to celebrate the completion of the refurbishment work and thank them for their help. I consulted Grace first and agreed the guest-list and menu and then sent out invitations. From the Manor House there would be Caitlin and myself, Grace and Gregory. I invited Jason, the overseer, Matthew Jamison, the head river bailiff and Andrew Green the farm manager.

I had ordered some wine uncorked for the evening and we sat outside on the new paved courtyard to drink before retiring to the dining room. I made a little speech, thanking them for their support during the changes and emphasising my wish that we should constantly try to raise the level of professionalism in all we did. Our task was to impress our guests in every possible way.

It started to get a little chilly as dusk fell and we moved into the dining room. The meal was delightful and the conversation flowed freely, as did the wine. It was a good evening and I felt it was a worth-while acknowledgement and thanks for their work and support.

When we retired, I was surprised to realise that Caitlin was exceedingly tipsy as she rarely drank. I helped her upstairs to our room where she became decidedly amorous and playful. That was no great surprise as, since our very first intimate liaison, she had always been forward in instigating nocturnal activities when we retired to bed. I knew that she was no longer starved of affection; I made certain of that, but she was ever keen to share her beautiful body with me. Tonight, under the influence of the wine, she was incorrigible and we made love every possible way into the small hours of the night. How I loved that girl.

It was tough to force myself from my bed the following morning but I knew that we had guests arriving and there was much to organise. I dressed, kissed Caitlin goodbye and was out as dawn broke.

Our next party of fishing guests arrived that day and we were ready for them. Matthew had continued to enlarge the size of the parties and, although it meant that we had to assemble every gillie from the Estate and several more helpers to support the rods, the arrangement was working well. Also, whether it was because of the hatched fry Matthew was reintroducing to the river or from some other cause, the number of fish seemed to be increasing. As always, I entertained our visitors to dinner and they were very complimentary about their changed surroundings as well as the quality of the fishing.

We had one of our best fishing seasons on record that summer, despite the greater numbers of visitors; it was helping to repay some of the investment I had spent on the Estate. I felt that we had created an aura of exclusivity and that visitors increasingly accepted that they were privileged in being allowed to be part of such a select assembly. We very quickly discovered that word of our new status spread from mouth to mouth and increased numbers sought to apply to join the parties.

John arrived home from university for the summer and, like everyone else, he was impressed with the magnificence of the changes which had taken place since his last visit. The following year was to be his last and he told me that there would be a graduation ceremony at the end which he would like me to attend. Apart from the adjoining estate at The Chase and my periodic trips to the market, I had not left the environs of the Estate in all my life. The thought of going to a city beyond the confines of Cumberland was quite terrifying and I cavilled, saying I would have to make that decision nearer the time.

We continued to make little family trips out in the pony and trap on Sunday afternoons. Caitlin and I would sit up front and drive the trap whilst Morag, assisted by John would ride in the rear entertaining the increasingly active twins. We visited many parts of the Estate including, one afternoon, my childhood home beside the river. I had not told John where we were going. He had not been there since he had left at the age of six but instantly recognised the place and told Morag about his early home and about his mother.

The assistant gamekeeper was in the cottage and I asked his permission for us to sit on the bench and for the twins to play around the house. There was a shallow beach just past the bend in the river and we took the twins there and allowed them to play at the water's edge, keeping a very watchful eye on them the whole time. They splashed about happily for some time but I could tell that Caitlin was anxious and fretful, lest they should venture too far into the water. After a little while I scooped them up and deposited them back in the trap, ready for home. We had many happy trips that summer, visiting different parts of the Estate.

On one such Sunday we visited the egg hatchery which Jack had developed. Whilst he was opening up 'Jack's Highway', Jack had continued to keep a proprietorial eye on the contraption but I had commissioned a young lad called Ahab to look after the hatchery. Ahab had been dropped on his head as a baby and he was a little retarded. However, Jack helped him to build a hut to live in and taught him how to place and turn the eggs at regular daily intervals. Even more important, he emphasised that the fire had to be kept alive day and night, and never be allowed to go out. I was a little anxious because, if the lad failed in his duty, an entire year's game might be wiped out and never hatch. We alerted everyone on the Estate within a five-mile radius to regularly call on Ahab to check that he was doing his job. In the event, he did it diligently and we reared a good percentage of chicks.

Caitlin and I lay in bed together in each-other's arms after one such Sunday outing. As usual, Caitlin was in a playful and naughty mood and completely exhausted me. The candle was still flickering at the bedside and I saw her start to make strange signs and gestures and protested, thinking that she meant "Again! Now!" Eventually I understood that she was telling me that she was expecting again. This time she had recognised the symptoms and had not needed to get confirmation from the village wives. I was delighted at the news and, together, we worked out that the baby would probably be due around the end of December. It would be a wonderful Christmas present.

Our prestigious guests arrived for the Glorious Twelfth. It was their first visit since we had completed the major refurbishments. As I had hoped and anticipated, they were totally smitten with the changes we had made and eulogised continually about the improvements. They loved 'Jack's Highway' and the impressive circular courtyard. They adored the new portico and marble hallway and they almost drooled over the changes to the dining and reception areas. The guest who had recommended Miss Tamsin Grey crowed continually that his recommendation had wrought such a wonderful transformation.

That first evening we took our pre-prandial beverages on the new paved courtyard before making our way inside where we dined in the splendour of the transformed dining room. The conversation was warm and convivial. Each guest went out of his way to assure me that they would be dispensing glowing recommendations to all their friends and contacts. That was a welcome endorsement.

And the shoot the following day was no anti-climax. Every self-respecting grouse for miles around turned up to offer itself as a sacrifice in the interests of the Estate. The day stayed fine, our visitors had unrivalled sport and welcomed the superb luncheon laid on for them in the covered barns. The food and drink were so plentiful that I had a little difficulty in rousing them from their torpor to return them to the afternoon's sport.

Again that evening we dined royally and, as I bade them farewell the following day, I knew that we had secured supporters who would continue to join us for years to come and to recommend the Manor House Estate wherever they went. The pattern of happy guests was repeated again and again over the following weeks.

Just before the Harvest celebration I spent some time with Gregory, going through the Estate accounts. Things were going well and income was up from all sources. Timber, milled flour and all excess farm produce was being sold outside the Estate and yielding some excellent profits. Income from increased fishing numbers and higher shoot fees had transformed the accounts and, since the builders had been released, costs were falling fast. I was pleased although Gregory told me that the Laird rarely looked at the accounts and showed very little interest in Estate affairs.

There was a special feeling about the Harvest supper that year. Everyone knew that it had been a successful year and that the Estate had taken a big step up in its facilities and presentation. They were proud of what they had achieved both as individuals and as a body. We were special. I arranged with Grace for us to serve the best and most abundant repast that had ever been offered at a Harvest supper and ensured that the barrels of beverage were the best and most abundant we could find. As always, Caitlin and I led the dancing and the twins went around endearing themselves to all and sundry and begging any tasty morsel they spied. The evening was a great success.

Our next guests arrived on the Monday but the morale of all our workers was sky-high and they in turn ensured the enjoyment of our visitors. Light rain in early October did little to dampen spirits on either side.

Quite suddenly and unexpectedly, Caitlin went in to labour in the second half of October; at least two months too early. I called two of the Estate ladies to come and help her and made myself scarce. Unable to keep away, however, I returned a couple of hours later. I was told that the baby was hopelessly premature and had not lived more than a few minutes. I had lost another baby.

They were still attending to Caitlin. I wandered off again and when I returned they were still unwilling to admit me. An hour later when they still resisted my request I over-rode them and entered her room, despite their protestations. Caitlin lay on the bed, pale and wan and decidedly exhausted. The bedclothes were bathed in blood and her women told me that Caitlin was haemorrhaging blood. I stood beside my beautiful woman and held her hand, but there was little else

I could do except to speak warm and loving words and bid her to recover.

I stayed at her side for three days, holding her hand, whilst life slowly ebbed from her. I felt a tiny squeeze of my hand just before she departed this life and left me. My world had ended and I wept like an abandoned child.

Eventually one of the women propelled me from the room into the kitchen and gave me a soothing beverage, whilst the other lady dealt with Caitlin's body. Later I wandered out into the dawn and walked and walked with no sense of direction. Eventually I found myself beside the river outside my childhood home. I sat and watched the river. I was not cleansed; I was not purified; I was not revived. My love had ended, and with it, my life. I imagined that the river had frozen and the waters had stopped.

I know not how long I sat there but when I eventually arose, dusk was gathering. I wondered disconsolately back to the Manor House. Caitlin's body had been laid out downstairs. I kissed her cold lips and retired to bed where exhaustion quickly claimed me into oblivion.

The following morning I went into the forest and dug a grave, then carried her in my arms and laid her in it. Could I have lain with her and covered us both with soil, I would have done so. For much of the day I sat beside her grave and wept over her, cursing whatever gods had ruled our destiny on the stupidity of the mistake they had made. My tears were as futile as my anger. I wept the soil into her grave with every ounce of love in my body, and left.

Chapter 17

When I finally pulled myself together, I went to visit the twins. It was pointless to try to communicate the loss of their mother to them. They were still too young to understand. Fortunately, Morag was their anchor point. She was their daily presence and although I regret that they felt my sadness, the presence of Morag was their rock. In a quiet moment I assured Morag that I needed her now, more than ever and wanted her to stay to care for the twins.

I went to talk to Jason and told him I wanted him to host our guests for a little while whilst I recovered. He had grown significantly since I had appointed him as overseer and I was confident that he would do a good job. He entertained our visitors for several weeks whilst I moped and railed at the injustice of Caitlin's death. However, as December broke I started to recover sufficiently to remember my responsibilities and act as host to our procession of guests.

I found it difficult to cope with the Manor House traditional Christmas celebrations without Caitlin at my side but, somehow, I struggled through. I hosted the children's Christmas present presentation in the Manor House and processed with them down to the Great Barn. I picked at my meal absent-mindedly and left as soon as decency allowed. It was hard.

At nights I lay and thought of my lovely lady. As a mute, I had never heard her voice but, with her departure, I seemed to hear her voice, again and again; loud and clear, and I treasured the sound and bade it come again. In my imagination, she said all of the things she could not say when alive. At night I would imagine her, playful and naughty as of old, saying the things for which her actions had never needed words. Oh! My love! My love! My love!

The New Year finally galvanized me into re-joining the human race. I had a business, an Estate to run. I had neglected it for too long. I took up the yoke again and accepted my responsibilities. I was the Estate Manager. With just four weeks of the season remaining, I threw myself back into the work and ensured that our guests had my total and undivided attention. Still oft-times, when our visitors had retired to their beds, I would creep out into the forest to stand beside her grave and tell her she was not forgotten.

That February it snowed, harder than it had for years and the snow stayed on the ground for almost a month. I took Morag and the twins out into the forest to play in the snow. They were nearly four years old and had not previously seen snow. They revelled in the experience and helped me to build a little person out of snow and we threw snowballs at each other. Soon, however, they started to feel chilled and Morag insisted that we return to the Manor House.

Ample fuel had been stacked in the dry against a cold winter and we had fires roaring throughout the house to keep us warm. As the freeze continued, however, I became concerned for some of the more elderly people on the Estate and I sent messages out through everyone in the area, asking them to keep an eye out for any who might be suffering. There were several cases and I sent out fuel and food to aid them. Sadly, one old retainer who had chosen to live deep in the forest was found too late, dead in his hut, frozen solid.

The thaw, when it finally arrived, was as dramatic as the snow. The ground was boggy and the river rose to dangerous levels. Fortunately, the work I had commissioned on raising the banks after the last flood held, and the river continued to pursue its ordained course. The Estate lands were always quick to drain and dried out well before the first of our visitors arrived for the fishing season.

I started to receive reports from around the Estate that we were being plagued by foxes. They were always a problem near the farms but the farmers were constantly on the alert and dealt with them promptly. Now they seemed to be right across the land and to have bred profusely over the last few years and were decimating the game. In the brief lull before our guests started to arrive I organised a series of hunts to try to bring the menace under control. Our land did not lend itself to the traditional mounted fox hunts. Instead, we walked for miles to where fox dens had been reported and spent hours digging them out. I know that Caitlin had regarded the process as cruel but the carnage they wreaked on the livestock on the Estate demanded action. We certainly reduced their numbers that spring, before the first of our guests arrived.

The first of our visitors started to arrive for the fishing. I had got to know many of them over the years and welcomed them back warmly. However, as the reputation of the Manor House spread by word of mouth, many new visitors appeared that year and had to be accorded every courtesy. It put a strain on our resources but the Estate rose to the challenge and I dare to claim that no guest left us disappointed at the sport or the entertainment. As I had hoped and planned, we were increasingly professional in our care and nothing was left to chance.

As summer progressed I visited Raphael, the overseer at The Chase, carefully avoiding the house itself. I was perfectly happy with my quiet life and had no wish to attract the attention of the hive. However, I did want to check on the conditions and game in anticipation of the coming season. Raphael had grown in stature since I had appointed him as overseer and was fully in charge of the game keeping. Conditions were perfect for the opening of the season and I looked forward to the arrival of our guests. He did mention that, as at the Manor House, there appeared to be a sudden resurgence in the number of foxes but we agreed to ignore them until after the shooting season.

It was a real pleasure to welcome back our distinguished guests for the Glorious Twelfth. We were old friends by now and settled into an easy relationship. One of them expressed mock-surprise that we had not redesigned the world again over the past year. I explained that my wife had died and it had hit me hard, temporarily robbing me of the drive for change. They were saddened to learn of Caitlin's passing.

As always, we dined well on that first evening and talked well into the night. Despite the hour, we were up early again the next morn and out on the grouse moors shortly after dawn. The beaters were in place, the sun had already appeared in the sky, melting the early morning mist and we had an unparalleled day's sport. The guests were in fine spirits as they were carried back to the Manor House on our special horse-drawn omnibus conveyance. We had a great celebration and a brilliant dinner that evening. Our guests lacked for nothing. They left the following morning, promising to return next year.

After they departed, it was time to prepare for our next visitors and the succession of guests continued right through to the Harvest supper which was always a big event on the Estate. I determined to make it a special event this year, celebrating the memory that Caitlin had been with me at the last supper. The twins, who were now four and a half, joined me at the top table, with Morag in attendance to maintain good order. The children were insufferably cute and little Caitlin went around the tables batting her eyelids at the men; they adored her. Her brother, Richard, seemed to play some similar trick with the ladies and the two of them could have charmed the birds out of the trees.

I was in a quandary on how to start the dancing as any partner I chose might have been misinterpreted. In the event

I arranged that I would dance with little Caitlin and Morag would dance with Richard. After a minute or two we would all split-up and each take a new partner into the dance. The children behaved impeccably and were much admired.

I had received a letter from John giving me details of his forthcoming graduation ceremony and making it very clear that he would be most disappointed if I did not attend. It was blackmail, but I had no alternative. I left on the morning after the Harvest supper, leaving Jason in charge of the Estate. I was terrified at the prospect of visiting a city as I had never been beyond our local market town since I was born. I walked to town and boarded the Post Chaise on which I had loaded John all those years ago on his first trip to boarding school.

The stagecoach left our local town and bounced along the rough unmetalled tracks into unfamiliar lands. We passed by lakes that I had never seen before then I slowly started to feel a distinct sense of loneliness and even terror as I saw the mountains of Cumberland disappear behind me. The journey took three days and we stopped at an inn each evening, reaching the city late on the third day. It was utterly frightening. I was surrounded by countless numbers of people whom I knew not and by huge buildings on every side. From where I alighted, I could not see a single tree.

Fortunately, John was there to meet me. He greeted me warmly then led me to the rather nice inn where he had reserved a room for me. We ate there that evening and I was glad not to have to brave the maze of streets which surrounded us. I had never experienced any problem in finding my way through the forests of Cumberland, but I was lost in those streets. We had an excellent meal together and talked long into the night. John somehow knew the pain I suffered at the loss of Caitlin and did not feel it a betrayal of Mary, his mother. He had been offered an appointment in Law Chambers in London and would soon be departing for there. I felt that it would be a long time before we saw each other again.

I begged John to collect me from the inn the following morning and conduct me to the ceremony. I sat in the very grand auditorium surrounded by more people than I had thought existed. John was attired in the magnificent robes and mortar board of a Doctor of Law and was the youngest person to qualify for the degree, by several years. The eminent professors filed onto the stage and the ceremony commenced. In due time John was called to the stage and presented with his certificate and I, his surrogate father, sat there bursting with pride. It was a very special moment.

I journeyed home again over the next three days and reached the Manor House with a huge sense of relief. The world was far too large for my liking and I had no intention of ever visiting it again.

A few days later was the anniversary of Caitlin's death. We had many guests that week and I was responsible for entertaining them but, when they had finally all retired for the night, I went out into the forest with a lantern and placed some flowers on her grave. A gentle breeze was blowing through the trees and I seemed to hear her silent voice whisper "Thank you".
Oh! How I struggled still to cope with her loss. My love! My love! My love!

The reputation of the quality of the sport and the lavishness of the entertainment at the Manor House Estate had spread and the number of guests continued to climb. I realised that I needed to review the number of senior managers on the Estate and possibly add to them to cope with the increasing workload.

Matthew Jamison, the Head Gillie seemed to be coping with the increased demand and Andrew Green, the Farm

Manager, had things very much under control. Jason had fully proved himself as Overseer and I promoted him to Head Gamekeeper. Dale Walter who I had helped to launch as an assistant gamekeeper a number of years before had proved to be a highly intelligent member of the staff. I promoted him to Overseer. I discussed with Grace her requirements for the household staff and we increased numbers, particularly below stairs and I recruited a youngster to help Gregory in his treasury work.

I felt desperately in need of a House Manager to handle the logistics of the comings and goings and needs of our guests. For the moment I had no solution to that problem.

I coped better that year with the Christmas celebrations. I deputised the twins to hand out the presents to the other Estate children, under Morag's watchful eye. I dispensed the drinks to the other residents and took the opportunity to talk with them all, particularly those I rarely saw. Afterwards we progressed down to the Great Barn and enjoyed a magnificent Christmas dinner.

Shooting recommenced at the beginning of January and continued throughout the month. In casual conversations with a number of guests I mentioned that I was looking for a House Manager. One guest told me that he was selling his house in the north in order to move to the other end of the country. He had a first-rate House Manager called Oliver who he would be happy to recommend to me. I asked him to send the fellow to me as soon as convenient.

I interviewed Oliver when he arrived. He had worked at several notable houses in the past and came with a string of impeccable references. I explained the job I wanted him to undertake. He was not there to entertain the guests; he was there to ensure that they were entertained. I needed him to manage the logistics of their arrival and departure, to work with Grace to ensure that accommodation was arranged, that they were expected at table and that transport was on hand when required. In short, I wished him to anticipate every need of our guests and see that they were met and exceeded. Oliver was happy with the brief and took up his post a few weeks later. He was as good as his reports and did the job to my complete satisfaction and eased my workload.

Chapter 18

After the last guest had departed at the end of January we breathed our annual sigh of relief and relaxed for a couple of months and turned our attention to breeding new flocks of chicks, without which there would be no shooting next year. I reviewed the Estate accounts with Gregory and was not surprised to find that we had had a most successful year financially. I spoke with Grace at length about her kingdom and we agreed that it was time to upgrade the crockery, cutlery, silverware and glassware used by our guests. Much of it had started to show signs of age with chips or tarnish. We had to ensure that our guests had the very best.

I sent a note to Raphael asking if he wanted assistance to cull his growing fox population. He replied that the Laird and Elizabeth had taken to horse and were out fox hunting on a regular basis. We were not required and instead, I visited every part of the Estate and every person on it.

As always, it was a joy to visit the farms and see what changes Andrew Green had wrought. The quality of the soil had been improved by his crop-rotation and application of manure and lime. The beasts in the fields were no longer sallow and sickly; they were strong and healthy. The crops showing through the ground were plentiful and the farm workers were happy, contented and proud of what they had achieved. The corn mill was operating successfully, as was the saw mill. The later had long-since dealt with the timber from 'Jack's Highway' and was now eating its way through timber from deeper in the forest. I asked who was managing which areas of forest to harvest and learned that Andrew had taken that task on himself and was also managing the replanting as appropriate.

Andrew had also diverted some river water into a culvert he had had dug. At its upper-reaches it supplied fresh water to the cottages and he had organised pipes to run water into the buildings. Lower down, the water supplied the needs of the cattle and further still was used for irrigation, as required. In his spare time he had also taken a woman. That was good news as it meant stability. He was settled.

I moved on to inspect other parts of the Estate. I had ordered some work on widening and draining one of the much-used bridleways and I was pleased to find that the work was nearly completed. I had also commissioned a small bridge to be built over a rather deep and lively stream and that was complete and should have no problem carrying the weight of a horse and loaded cart. I called on every woodsman and assistant gamekeeper on the Estate and on The Chase and thanked them for their work. I checked on the hatchery which was still in full production. Ahab was in attendance and proud that he had never allowed the fire to go out. He told me that he had built up a good stock of firewood before the winter. During the snows he had actually slept inside the hatchery for the entire month. This was partly to avoid freezing to death but also to ensure that the fire never went out. I told him he had done a good job and he preened himself.

The year continued to turn. We celebrated the twins fifth birthday. I asked Morag to find someone who could teach them to read and write. Morag was now seventeen and, to my surprise, she told me that she had learned from her parents before they died and that she had continued reading copiously from the Manor House library. She had already started to teach the children some simple reading and writing and would gladly continue the task.

The first of our fishing parties arrived and I became immediately aware of the benefit the appointment of Oliver had brought. He had an excellent eye for detail. He briefed himself well before the arrival of each party and ensured with almost mechanistic precision that everything was in order for them. No detail escaped his attention and I was quickly able to leave the detailed arrangements in his hands. He stationed himself at a desk in the front entrance hall and guests soon came to realise that anything they required would be resolved through a quick word with Oliver. I was free to entertain our visitors.

I was out on the river with one of our parties when I received a message from Raphael that there had been an accident at The Chase. There were no further details so I called for a horse and made my way to Raphael's cottage fearful of what I might find.

He told me that the Laird and Elizabeth had been out fox hunting on their fine horses, together with friends and dogs. They had raced each other towards a ditch; Elizabeth arrived there first and went to jump the ditch but the horse hesitated and she was thrown. One observer reported hearing the sickening crack as her neck broke. She was dead immediately.

My heart went out to him. I had lost two wives and knew the pain. I was in a quandary; it was unlikely that he would welcome my condolences at this moment and, in any case, he clearly had friends about. It seemed unlikely that his bride would have the simple woodland burial I had accorded to both mine. It was more likely to be a proper church affair and that he would seek the services of a parson. That would take time. I decided to wait until the burial and asked Raphael to let me know as soon as he heard the arrangements. In the meantime, I would send a formal note of condolence.

I sent the note as soon as I returned to the Manor House. Two days later I received a reply thanking me for my note. It went on to tell me that the burial would be at the tiny chapel belonging to the Manor House. He had summoned a parson from a distant parish and hoped that the ceremony would be on the coming Friday. He asked me to arrange for a grave to be dug adjacent to those of his mother and father. I replied, acknowledging the request and then organised for the chapel to be cleaned thoroughly and for the grave to be dug.

We had a party of guests who were due to depart on Friday morning. I went through the details meticulously with Oliver and asked him to orchestrate their departure as efficiently as possible to avoid any overlap with the funeral. The Laird had given no indication that the wake meal was to be at the Manor House but I alerted Grace against the possibility, asking her to arrange a cold repast which could quickly be made available. I also told her that I wanted as many as possible of the servants to form a guard of honour as the coffin was carried into the chapel.

We had not been given a time so I posted one person on a horse where he would have a good view to see when the cortege left The Chase. He was then to ride back and alert us so that everyone would be in place for their arrival. When nothing had appeared by mid-afternoon, I sent another rider to The Chase to make enquiries. The funeral had been delayed until the Saturday morning and we stood-down.

We were back in place early on the Saturday morning and our look-out rode back to tell us that the cortege was on its way. We monitored its progress and, when it was within twenty minutes, I had the guard of honour in place. They arrived at the entrance to the chapel, the Laird looked strangely at the guard of honour in their uniforms then led the coffin into the chapel, followed by a party which seemed to consist of their house guests and some servants. I followed the last of them but found the doors of the chapel closed in my face. Somewhat embarrassed, I pushed my way inside.

The service was simple and mercifully brief and the funeral party left the chapel and gathered at the graveside. The parson intoned blessings and benedictions, the coffin was lowered into the grave and soil was scattered over it. The Laird led the party back to the carriages and they departed without him once acknowledging my presence. I thought this strange.

I led our party back to the Great Barn where food had been laid out on tables. I announced that this was the Manor House wake for the departed wife of the Laird, and bid them feast. They did not need telling twice.

Life at the Manor House returned to normal and fishing parties came and went. Since the appointment of Oliver, our well-oiled machine ran more smoothly than ever. My objective was to project an aura where every guest felt that they were special and that they had received our undivided attention. For the most part I believe that we achieved that objective. Whether as a result of Matthew's fish hatchery or for some other reason, the fishing remained excellent and the earlier definition of 'good' stands and 'bad' stands on the river, no longer seemed relevant. All the fishing was good and our guests invariably enjoyed their visit and the fishing, as well as the entertainment which we lavished upon them in the evenings.

Our fishing season drew to a close and I checked the arrangements for the start of the shooting season. As usual, it was to be staged on the grouse moors of The Chase lands. Raphael had really risen to his task and both the conditions and the amount of game were perfect and I knew that our distinguished guests would be pleased.

Chapter 19

We had heard nothing from the Laird since Elizabeth had been laid to rest some months ago. Possibly the sound of the shoot on the Chase moors reminded him of our existence and Gregory received a summons to take the Manor House books across to him for examination. Gregory and I had worked closely together over recent years and he came to me troubled, on his return from visiting the Laird. He had been challenged repeatedly over the levels of expenditure for the various works I had commissioned on the Estate. Gregory had valiantly protested that the costs had vastly increased the income but the Laird had not been satisfied. He had ordered that I should attend him to explain.

I did so at the earliest opportunity and was attacked immediately on the 'frivolous' expenditure. I explained that we had deliberately set out to raise the standards for our guests. I pointed out that it had achieved the planned results and I reminded the Laird that he had approved the expenditure. This he denied vehemently. He accused me of misuse of Estate money and told me he would visit the Estate on the following morning for a fuller explanation.

He had not visited the Manor House since he and Elizabeth had departed for The Chase. When he arrived the following morning and saw the huge extent of the changes since his last visit, he was incandescent, shouting and swearing at the ridiculous work and the totally unnecessary expenditure. He refused to see the work as improvements and would not accept that they had resulted in increasing numbers of guests or in raising their level of satisfaction in their visits. He was implacable.

Before he left, he announced that he would move back to the Manor House so that he could prevent any further profligate misuse of funds. He was curt with me and it was clear that our relationship had changed. I imagined that to the sudden demise of Elizabeth must be attributed this sudden and violent change in his nature and demeanour. It was plain that our relationship was going to be different. As a precaution, I moved Morag and the twins out of the Manor House and installed them in the now-empty cottage that Mary and I had occupied when we first moved to the Estate office.

The Laird duly moved back in to the Manor House two days later and I noticed that he spent several seconds examining the statue in the driveway, before entering the house. I saw him looking from the statue to me as though he could see the parallel between us. I had always avoided occupying the Master bedroom in the Manor House and knew now that it had been wise.

We had shooting guests to entertain that evening and I asked Oliver to include seats for both the Laird and myself. I accompanied the guests on their shoot and they had some excellent sport. We returned to the Manor House, dressed for dinner and gathered on the paved courtyard for drinks. The Laird immediately launched into a tirade at the unnecessary cost of the paved courtyard; why could we not gather in the lounge as we had always done. I refused to rise to the bait and let him rant on but our guests started to look decidedly uncomfortable.

The following morning the Laird again chose to attack me about all the stupid and unnecessary alterations which had been introduced. As near as makes no difference he started to accuse me of embezzlement of his funds. I had always been scrupulously honest and cavilled. I raised my voice to refute the charge and asked why he could not see that the changes had been done for the benefit of the Estate and the enjoyment of guests.

He shouted at the top of his voice "How dare you speak to me like that? Get out of this house." So I did.

I went round to see Jason in MacTavish's old house and told him how the land lay. I suggested to him that the Laird would probably be looking to him to support his view that I had been a poor steward and that it would be in his interests to accept the view and not to disagree. He agreed to let me use one of his bedrooms for a few nights, whilst I saw how the wind blew. I stayed there and maintained a low profile avoiding any contact with the Laird.

When Jason returned from a meeting with the Laird he told me that his position as Head Gamekeeper had been confirmed. The Laird had announced that I had been dismissed and that he would assume the role of Estate Manager once more. A few days later we learned that he had reviewed the list of Estate servants with Gregory. Over twenty people had been summarily dismissed from service, including Oliver.

I took myself off to the farms to see Andrew Green with whom I had long-since established a close friendship. I explained to him how things lay and asked for a favour. Morag had come from one of his cottages; did he have a spare cottage to which she could return, together with my twins. I felt they could all hide there, undetected. Andrew was happy to oblige and a couple of days later I led Morag and the twins to their new home.

Whilst it was absolutely true that I had never embezzled a farthing from the Estate, I had received many generous tips from grateful guests and had saved them carefully and had a tidy sum. I divided the money up and gave two-thirds to Morag to look after herself and the children and kept the remaining third against my uncertain future. I trusted Morag totally and entertained no doubts that she would faithfully care for my bairns.

I returned to Jason's house where he brought me up to date on moves within the Manor House. The Laird had continued to decimate the number of Estate servants. There had also been an unfortunate fracas with a group of guests who had felt that they had not received the care and attention they had grown to expect from the Manor House Estate. They had apparently been told that, if they didn't like it, they should not bother to come back. It saddened me.

Jason told me that the assistant gamekeeper who had occupied my childhood home beside the river had left earlier in the year and that he was also without a woodsman for the same part of the forest. He was looking for a replacement. I leapt at the news. I told him that I would move there immediately and take up the dual posts but that he should list me down under another name so that the Laird would not be aware of my existence.

That evening I took my axe, my shotgun and a few other possessions and walked to the river. The cottage was in a poor state of repair. Parts of the thatched roof had collapsed and the door stood at a crazy angle on its hinges. Major repairs would take time. For tonight I cleared an area of floor and covered it with fresh bracken for a bed and lay down to sleep. For the first time in many years I was lulled by the song of my river maiden singing to me and I slept soundly.

I was home.

In the morning I drank water from the river, ate some berries and nuts from the woods and then got to work to make my cottage habitable again. I cleaned the rubbish and fallen thatch, fitted a few new roof supports and re-thatched the roof. The damage was not as extreme as it had first appeared. I fixed the door and then made myself a pallet to sleep upon. As evening approached I tickled a very large trout from the river and cooked it on a spit over an open fire. I ate it with some plants and herbs I had gathered from the woods. It was a feast and I adjourned to my new bed well satisfied.

I knew that I needed a number of essential items from the market to enable me to survive in the cottage. The first priorities included a cooking pot, plates, beakers, cutlery and blankets as well as essentials such as flour and salt. I set out early the next morning for the town. I set some traps for game as I left in the hope that I might have something with which to christen my new cooking pot when I returned.

I used a circuitous route as I wanted to avoid meeting with anyone on the Estate. I felt at this early stage that the fewer people who knew about my continued presence in the forest, the better. I did not wish to come to the attention of the Laird with whom my once-convivial relationship had clearly ended. I ruminated on the matter as I walked. Although I was deeply saddened by the death of each of my wives, I believed that the experiences had softened me, made me gentler and more considerate. It appeared that the death of Elizabeth had had the opposite effect. It had made him bitter and vindictive and had affected his judgement. He was implacable. I cared little that I had fallen from the throne of grace but I was deeply saddened that it was adversely affecting the smooth running of the Estate.

I did not tarry when I reached town, lest I should meet others from the Estate. Instead, I made my purchases quickly and was back on my way before most of the town had awoken. Again, I went quietly and avoided the main areas of habitation although I only narrowly avoided being seen by one of the woodsmen. I hid behind a tree for several minutes until he had gone his way.

Back at the cottage I shed my burdens before gathering some wood to burn and lit the range. I found that I had snared a rabbit and a pheasant and prepared them for the pot. Whilst they were cooking I continued with work on the cottage. I made a stool and a small table at which to eat. By the time the meal was ready I felt I had all the comforts of home. I finished my meal, tidied up and went outside to sit on my bench which had survived all the changes.

For all the trauma taking place on the Estate, I was at peace with the world, and my world was peaceful. I sat and watched the river and listened to its siren song.

Chapter 20

Have you ever sat and watched a river? Have you seen how the water twists and turns, halts in the quiet eddies beside the bank, catches in a branch of the overhanging tree then frees itself and rushes on to catch up with the rest of the stream? It is cathartic is a river. It cleanses the soul. It seems to purify the blood and still the turmoil of the mind as it rushes past, carrying all ills away to leave one washed and purified. In its passing, no moment can ever be repeated. No single droplet of water will ever pass that way again. You can watch it for ever, and then watch it some more.

The sound too is hypnotic, mesmeric, compelling: it burbles and gurgles its song as it bounces across the stones and trips over itself in its headlong rush to oblivion. The babbling brook has a music of its own, a song which finds an echo in the soul. It calls, like a Lorelai siren maiden, her hypnotising voice luring the listener to join her in her watery bed. It draws one on, lulling the senses deeper and deeper into a peaceful repose. I was born beside this river and our lives were inextricably bound together. It was part of me and I seemed to carry its eternal and compelling song within me no matter how far from its banks I roamed. Here was my home.

In the peace of that evening hour I felt content, relaxed and renewed. I was a rich man.

I had told Jason that I would act as woodsman and assistant gamekeeper in my section of the forest, in return for my home. On the morrow I took my axe and went out to survey my plot. It was in a sorry state and had not been tended for several months. There was so much to be done that I wandered round for the best part of an hour, simply trying to prioritise the order in which I should tackle things. I decided that, for the future of the shooting, I should begin with the game. I rounded-up pheasants and partridges into their enclosure so that I could start a daily collection of eggs. I would then build my own little hatchery and start to breed new flocks.

I inspected the main bridleways and found that several were blocked by fallen trees and all of them needed work. I hefted my axe and set to work, biting into the wood with practiced strokes. I was surprised to find what hard work it was, then remembered that it was several years since this had been my daily routine. By the end of the day my muscles ached as they had not done for a long time. I collected game from the traps I had set and made my weary way back to the cottage.

And so the pattern was set for my new life. Each day I would set out for some area of my patch and work on restoring it to order. I built the intended hatchery, gathered eggs and started to incubate them. After three weeks, tiny chicks started to hatch and I was pleased with the success of again promoting new life. There was a lifetime of work to be done in the forest but, after three months I started to feel that I was again making a difference. I thought of the pride my father had always taken in his work and felt a debt of gratitude to him.

I was sitting on the bench one evening after work when I heard a horse approaching. I hid myself but emerged when I realised that it was Jason. He had been concerned that I had not appeared for three months to collect my wages and had brought it out to me. He obviously thought that harm had come to me. I invited him to join me on the bench and we talked for a long time. For my part I was very happy with my 'new' life and offered to show him the progress I was making.

For his part, Jason was distraught over developments at the Manor House. The Laird was becoming increasingly irrational and making decisions which were clearly not in the interests of the Estate. Servants were being fired at will and those remaining lived in fear for their livelihood. Guests were disgruntled at the treatment they were receiving and threatening not to return. After all the wonderful work which had been done on developing the Estate over the past few years, it was heart-breaking. I knew that there was nothing I could do to help.

On a happier note, Jason told me he had been to see Andrew Green at the farms. Andrew had mostly escaped the ire of the Laird and was continuing to plough his own furrow. Whilst there, Jason had called on Morag and the children and found them to be fit and well. I longed to see them and spend time with them but, whilst the wind lay in the current quarter, I deemed it best that neither they nor I should be discovered. I had little need of money for the present and asked Jason to give the money and my future wages to Morag and the children, for their care.

Another evening when I sat eating my evening meal there was a shout from without. I opened the door to find my old friend Mitch, the assistant gamekeeper. I invited him in and offered him a plate of dinner, which he accepted gladly. He wolfed it down and asked for more, then had the cheek to tell me that it was very nice, but not as good as Mary's. He was right, of course.

He told me he had noticed that things were starting to improve in this part of the forest and wandered who was responsible. He had been told that I had gone and was surprised when I had opened the door to him. We discussed the problems on the Estate and he relayed several new tales of atrocities. I asked him to keep my presence secret so that I could avoid the wraith of the Laird. Mitch agreed and often popped in for dinner after that, keeping me abreast of news.

I worked hard in the forest to earn my keep. I had reared a respectable number of chicks and looked after them. I had started to make a good impression on the woodland and bridle paths. By now, my muscles were toned again and I could deal with a day's work without discomfort.

After I had been back at the cottage for about nine months, Jason again visited me. He brought letters from John with lots of news on how he was enjoying life in London and telling me of his work. I had not told him about my fall from grace but resolved to do so. I scribbled a quick note to him as we talked and asked Jason to post it for me.

Jason told me that the Laird had suffered what the medics termed a 'mental breakdown' which they thought resulted from the stress of running the Estate. He had not left his bed for six weeks and refused to see anyone. His maid had reported that the only coherent thing he seemed to say was to call out my name, again and again, apparently asking to see me. No one in the household knew where I was but, as soon as Jason had heard, he had brought the news to me. "Would I come to see him?"
"No!"

Since my departure from the Manor House I had enjoyed infinite peace and quiet in the environ of my own private heaven. I was content with my lot. I had no desire to taste again the fruits of civilisation or success. I was home; this was my river.

When Jason left I wandered over to my vegetable garden and punished some weeds for daring to invade my tiny kingdom. Perhaps, after all, I was tempted to visit the Laird, if only for old-time sake.

Jason visited me yet again, a few weeks later. The organisation of the Estate was declining into chaos. The laird was not improved but, through his maid, had sent a message to Jason, asking if he knew where I was. Jason had prevaricated and replied that he would make enquiries. The message from the Laird was that he needed my help. I again declined and punished more weeds when he had departed.

I continued to work conscientiously on my part of the forest. I had been back for nearly a year and I knew that I was starting to make a real impression, both as a woodsman and a gamekeeper. Mitch often dropped in unannounced at dinner time and I enjoyed his company. He kept me up to date with affairs on the Estate and always had some amusing anecdote to share.

Mitch was ageing fast and his fear was that the caring support of ageing workers which had been part of the Estate style in the past, might no longer apply to him in his dotage. That saddened me as I had sought to manage the Estate affairs with compassion. It occurred to me that I too might find myself in similar straights at some future time. I still had most of the one-third of the money I had saved from my 'fat years' as Head Gamekeeper and Estate Manager, but that would not last for ever. I thought on the subject often as I worked in the forest following our conversation.

Possibly my favourite time of the week was Sunday afternoons. I would make and enjoy a generous luncheon, after which I would sit on my bench and watch the river as it flowed from the beginning of time towards eternity. I loved the scene and its parable of life. My river and my life.

One Sunday after I had been home for about a year, I was sitting, dozing in the afternoon sunshine when I heard the unmistakable sound of cartwheels and a harness. I was tempted to hide but was slow to do so and a pony and trap hove into view. It was driven by Jason but, in the back, enveloped in blankets, sat the Laird. Jason made gestures indicating apologies but explained that the Laird had suffered a stroke and was partially paralysed. His speech was blurred, but discernible. Over the past few weeks he had repeatedly called my name and asked to see me and speak with me.

I did not know how to react. I had no desire ever again to see or to speak with the Laird but his arrival had robbed me of choice. He was here. Jason helped him down from the trap and led him into my cottage, then went out to tend to the horse. I entered the cottage and closed the door behind me. I had not sought him but I was clearly trapped.

"Richard," the Laird ventured. He had not called me that for many moons and I liked the sound of it. He continued "I have made a massive mess of things and I am come to apologise. The death of Elizabeth scored me deeply and, although it is no excuse, I believe I have been mentally unstable ever since. I became paranoid about many things, money, your effortless success and what I perceived as the disloyalty of my servants. I know now that you made unprecedented improvements to the appearance and the running of the Estate and my vilification of you was totally unforgivable. I was jealous of your success and the loyalty you engendered. I'm sorry and I want you to come back and run the Estate."

I told him that I was happy where I was. I had enjoyed unparalleled peace and solitude since my eviction and I had no wish to return. He persevered, telling me that he needed me; the servants needed me; the Estate needed me. I was unmoved.

"You may not be aware but John has corresponded with me ever since he first went to boarding school and, like you, I am proud of what he has achieved. He has written to me saying that he has only recently learned of my illness and of the problems which have arisen on the Estate as a result. He has scourged me roundly for my stupidity. I would not accept such abuse from anyone else but, because I respect him, his words are the first ones to breach my defence of pride and anger. That is why I am here; I know that he is correct and I want to bring this madness to a close. Last evening, Grace and Gregory came to see me, asking to be released from my service. I refused them permission to leave, as I know that any remaining semblance of organisation would collapse on their departure, but it was the final straw. Please come back."

In a reply which would certainly have had me fired in the past, I told him simply that I could not trust him not to turn against me again at some future time and I did not need the uncertainty or the stress of the job.

He replied "I have thought of that, Richard, and your scepticism is fully warranted, I have acted unpardonably. I have recently suffered a stroke and my doctors tell me that I may have another at any time and that the next one could be fatal. I have no living relatives and no issue to leave the Estate to when I die. I intend to retire back to The Chase where I trust the pressures will be lessened and I shall play no part in the running of the Estate."

"This is my proposal. I shall have an irrevocable deed drawn up ceding my title of Laird to you. The entire Manor House and Estate will be gifted to you absolutely in perpetuity. I shall reserve one quarter of the annual profits of the Estate to maintain my household at The Chase during my lifetime. Upon my death, The Chase will be bequeathed to John, absolutely."

He paused for breath. I was silent, stunned, and said nothing.
Fearing that I was about to reject his offer he turned to me pleadingly, "Please Richard, help me end this madness. I need you. I know of no one else who can do the job."
Still I said nothing. This was a massive and unsought for intrusion on my life and I needed time before coming to any decision.

Finally I spoke. "I am extremely happy with my life here and I am not at all certain that I wish to surrender my peace and tranquillity for a task which I know will be daunting. Go ahead and ask your lawyers to draw up the documents. I will write to ask John if he is able to take time out to come peruse the details and to advise me and help me. After that, I will give you my decision."

The Laird seemed satisfied with that and we parted. Jason helped him back into the trap and they drove off.

Oh! How the fickle wheel of fortune turns.

I sat down and wrote to John soliciting his help in making the decision. The following morning I was too confused to work in the forest so I walked into town and delivered the letter to the post house in person.

On the way back I took a long detour to the farms. I was now discovered so there was little point in continuing to hide. Andrew welcomed me warmly. He had largely escaped the notice or the wrath of the Laird but regaled me with many sad stories from the Manor House part of the Estate. My real purpose in calling at the farms was to visit my children and Morag and Andrew led me to their cottage. The twins, who were now seven years old, welcomed me lovingly and we spent a wonderful two hours talking, playing and reminiscing. However, the big surprise was Morag. She was now nineteen and had turned into a very lovely young woman. I had to struggle to avoid staring at her. I reminded myself that I was more than twice her age.

I made careful enquiries on both the health and the education of the children and was assured that both were good. I also wanted to be certain that they were coping financially. Morag told me that the regular payment she was receiving for my wages was sufficient for their daily needs and she had spent very little of the savings I had left with her. The only time she normally used any of that money was to acquire material to make them clothes.

Before I left I told them where I had been living and added that, now the Laird knew where I lived, I hoped to be freer to travel about the Estate and visit them more often. I said nothing about the Laird's proposal as I was still most unsure.

Two weeks later, John turned up at my cottage door. I thought he had done extraordinarily well to find his way there after all these years but he confessed that Jason had put him on the right road. John had collected the documents from the Laird as he passed the Manor House and had brought them with him. We talked long into the night, firstly catching up on the news. He was thoroughly enjoying his life in London. He had already received a promotion within the law firm and was earning good money. He remonstrated with me for not telling him of my changed circumstances earlier as he would gladly have sent funds to help me. I made it clear to him that the past year had been wonderful for me and that I lacked for nothing.

He went on to read the legal documents out loud and to interpret them as he did so. It all seemed unequivocal. I was to be named Laird and the entire Estate was to be gifted to me as soon as we signed the documents. One quarter of the profits would go to the Laird at The Chase during his lifetime, to maintain his household there. On his death, The Chase became John's property.

John told me that he was in a difficult position because of this last part of the deed. He could not pretend to be impartial and insisted that we could only proceed if I was prepared to take up the burden of running the Estate again. I was still undecided on this. John told me that he had taken time to have a good look round at activities in the centre. He was appalled at what he had seen and suggested that I should accompany him there to see for myself. He added that he saw the task as daunting, but believed that my automatic reaction would be to roll my sleeves up and insist on resolving the problems. I had to agree that seeing the situation for myself would help me to make the decision, one way or the other.

We supped together that evening and then watched the river until it got dark. I made a bed up for him in his old bedroom although, somehow, it seemed not to fit him quite as well as when he had been six years old but it had a special feel to have him back in the cottage. On the morrow we made our way together to the Estate office and then to the Manor House.

John had been correct. Like him, I was appalled at what I saw. There was neglect and waste in every direction. Some of it might take years to sort out but much of it was superficial and could be corrected quickly. I looked about for someone to ask but could not see a soul. Suddenly I realised the problem; they were hiding, they were afraid. Just as I had chosen to hide myself from being noticed for the past year, every employee was maintaining a low profile and keeping below the parapet, lest they should be noticed and picked on. I could solve that problem in a day.

We announced ourselves at the Manor House and were ushered into the library to see the Laird, who was looking gaunt and sickly. He was accompanied by his lawyer and we introduced ourselves all round. I was asked if I had decided to proceed but deferred to John who wanted a few points in the deeds clarified. This was quickly accomplished, without opposition. John confirmed that the title deeds to the Estate had been produced and he checked them carefully. He asked to see the accounts of the Estate so that we could know what funds remained. The Laird confessed with some embarrassment that they were sadly depleted since my departure. He suggested that one quarter of the remaining funds should go with him to The Chase to maintain his household for the first year, whilst awaiting the first share of profits. That seemed reasonable although the remaining sum was much less than I would have liked with which to commence the battle ahead.

Whilst he was doing this, the Laird spoke. "Richard, because of my past misbehaviour I want to be totally clear what this means. If we proceed, you will be the absolute ruler of this demesne. I shall retire to The Chase and will have no further involvement here. I shall retain my airs and graces at The Chase but here you will be the Laird and master and you may address me by my given name, Jonathan. Now, are you willing to accept the burden of my gross mismanagement over the past year?" I looked at John who nodded and I gave my acceptance.

Grace and Gregory were summoned to the room and we each made our signature on the documents and they witnessed the signing. The Laird, or should I say Jonathan, opened a bottle of Madera wine but asked John to pour a glass for each of us as his hands were far from steady. He raised his glass in a toast to the Manor House Estate and to its new Laird, long life and happiness.

Jonathan announced that his effects were already packed and loaded onto a cart. He asked for the cart to be brought round to the front and he and his lawyer climbed aboard and were away. How could this possibly be real? I, Richard the woodsman was the Laird of the Manor.

John pumped my hand in congratulations and Grace and Gregory made touching little speeches on how dreadful things had been and how glad they were to see me returned. I told Grace that I would like her to organise a dinner in the Great Barn this coming Saturday evening and I asked Gregory to see that invitations were sent to everyone on the Estate. I also asked him to have a pony and cart sent down to Andrew Green at the farms, with a note asking him to load

Morag and the twins aboard and return them to me as soon as possible. I asked if either of them knew where Oliver had gone to. It transpired that Grace and Oliver had befriended each other and that she knew where he was staying. I asked her to write to him urgently and invite him to return, with my personal guarantee that things had changed.

Chapter 21

Grace and Gregory left us and I poured us each a second glass of Madera and thanked John for his help. He then asked the question I was dreading. "Where do you intend to start?" I freely admitted that I had no idea. When I had last transformed the affairs of the Estate, the changes had been incremental, one at a time. Now, everything needed doing and it needed doing immediately. I told him that the method which had always worked for me was to go around and see everything and talk to everyone. I would plan to do the same again now.

"Come on," I said. "Let's start now by spending the afternoon wandering around the Estate office and places nearby and talking to people. Let's see what we can learn."

Although many people had left the Estate over the past year, there was hardly anyone new. This meant that everyone knew me and I was welcomed back repeatedly with the wish that they hoped I could sort things out again. Rumours had already started to circulate that the Laird had left the Estate and the news was greeted with universal joy and relief. I quizzed everyone I met about what was wrong, and the problems they were experiencing. I learned a lot that afternoon.

We left the offices and met up with several of the servants returning from their day's work. I talked with each one of them and sought to learn their concerns. They delighted in my return and talked to me freely. They knew me of old and they knew me to be fair and compassionate.

As dusk descended we crossed back towards the Manor House. As we entered the gate a pony and trap caught up with us. It was Morag and the twins. We helped them down and I looked at John. He was staring at Morag and she at him. I swear that I heard the spark of static that passed between them. I realised what similar tastes we had; first

Caitlin, now Morag. But John was no longer a shy and awkward youth, he was a grown man and he quickly recovered himself and made polite conversation, but I could see that he was smitten. I was not surprised; she really had become a most attractive young woman. I devoted my attention to the children and welcomed them into their 'new' home. I suspect that we had all lost track of the number of times they had come and gone.

Grace organised some miracles for us and we had a most delightful family party in the main dining room that evening with lots of fun and laughter. John and Morag joined in occasionally but spent most of the meal gazing into each other's eyes. The old nursery was quickly prepared to receive Morag and the twins although I realised that my bairns would soon need larger beds and also that Morag would need her own room and privacy.

Tonight, for the very first time, I slept in the Master Bedroom. It was right; I was the master of the house and the Estate. My only regret was that Caitlin was not there to share it with me although I was certain that I would have had little sleep had she been there.
Oh! How I still missed her. My love; my love; my love.

I had already visited the farms and spoken with Andrew and I decided to leave a more extensive tour of the Estate until after Saturday. Instead, I spent most of the day talking with Jason and Matthew Jamison. I invited John to join me but he said that he would be happy to help Morag to settle the twins into some sort of routine. Why was I not surprised?

Matthew had been largely left to get on with organising his own fate on the fishing side of the business. Where he had been let down was on the entertainment side. It had formerly been lavish and its very opulence had been part of the attraction for our visitors. Over the past year they had been snubbed or ignored and had made it clear that they disliked the change. I assured him this was to revert immediately and every guest would receive our personal attention. I asked him to liaise with Grace on the programme. I would support him fully.

Jason's problems were more deep-seated. Jonathan (as I was now allowed to call him) had studiously neglected the husbandry of the forest and game keeping and there had been few or conflicting instructions to woodsmen and assistant gamekeepers. The excellence of the sport that we had engendered and nurtured had been lost in mediocrity. More important was the fact that the care and attention of our guests had disappeared and they had not been treated as 'special'. They had deserted us in droves. I assured him that all guests visiting for the shoots would have my personal attention and we would seek to repair the damage as quickly as we could. Again, I asked him to liaise with Grace to coordinate the diaries.

A great deal hung on the success of our impromptu dinner in the Great Barn on Saturday and I carefully rehearsed my speech. The barn was full to capacity when I arrived and I had ordered that the food and the cider and mead should flow freely before I assailed their ears. It worked well and when I rose to speak there was absolute silence.

I began by excusing the actions of the Laird. He had been totally shattered by the sudden death of his wife and spent the past year in a nightmare of regrets and had not been himself. I paralleled this with my own loss of two wives and how I understood his pain and misery. I told them that the Laird had left the Estate for good and that I was now their new Laird. In an attempt at humour I reminded them that this gave me absolute power over their lives; I was entitled to beat them three times each day and I intended to do so. Would they please line up outside my door at the end of the evening.

I returned to humility, noting that many of them had hidden themselves from the Laird to avoid his wrath and attention. I had done the same; I had hidden in the forest and returned to my work as a woodsman and assistant gamekeeper and had avoided the Laird. I was responsible for the mess we were now in and I apologised to them abjectly. I had let them down and the Estate was in a sorry state because of my neglect. I had returned and was ashamed of how our once-great enterprise had floundered. A year ago, we were the best Estate in our part of the country.

And then I spoke of the future. "My dream is that we will regain our place; we will once more be seen as the leading Estate for country sports; we will make every single one of our guests believe that they are the most important visitor in our whole year; that they are loved; that they are special and that we care. I want us to be known for excellence, excellence in everything we do. I want that to be our watchword and for no guest ever to leave our Estate without knowing that here they have enjoyed that excellence.
But I cannot do it alone, I need your help".

"Over the next few weeks I hope to visit almost every single one of you. I want you to tell me what I can do to help you and improve the quality of your life; and I want you to tell me what you can do to make the Manor House Estate not just great again, but the very best."

I raised my glass and proposed a toast to them all, the best bunch of people I could possibly wish to work with. I sat down to some genuine applause. The music struck–up and I took my daughter, Caitlin, to the dance floor. Morag took Richard although I noticed that after a few rounds of the floor, John excused him and danced with Morag for the rest of the evening.

The following morning I met with Gregory and asked for a full discussion on the finances of the Estate. After the brilliant state they had been in a year ago, they were a decided disappointment. We needed to rebuild our income as quickly as possible. I asked him to write to all our long-term visitors in my name and I dictated the outline of a letter. I apologised that I had not been present to greet them in the last year and also that the Laird had been extremely unwell following the death of his wife. I told them that we were preparing a special welcome for them this year to compensate for any disappointment and that we looked forward to seeing them. Not all our previous guests returned but there were sufficient and we went out of our way to fulfil our promise.

I next spoke with Grace. She had penned a letter to Oliver, as promised, and I sincerely hoped it would reap a positive response. We spent some time going through the forward diary and she was helpful in identifying guests whom she thought had been disappointed with their last visit. I asked her to work closely with Jason and Matthew and ensure that our guests had a wonderful visit this year.

John was due to leave for London that afternoon and I arranged transport to the town for him. I had enjoyed his company and asked that he visit us again as soon as he could. I avoided witnessing his parting from Morag but thought that she might well prove to be the most potent lure to draw him back again.

The following morning I set out to fulfil my promise to try to visit everyone on the Estate. I called first on each of the assistant gamekeepers and woodsmen. It was easy for me to relate to them as it was a world I understood and loved. I was also able to evaluate the livestock in their sector and the readiness of their territory to host shoots. Most of them were fairly happy with their lot in life but I was careful to enquire of each one of them. In truth, all they needed was support and leadership.

With Matthew's agreement, I tried to call on each water bailiff to solicit their views. Most simply wanted a quiet life and, in truth, they were hardly stretched.

I visited Raphael on The Chase estate and talked to him and his assistants. They had been largely untouched by Jonathan's irascible outbursts and they were fully ready for the season ahead. We toured their moors and I identified the next area of moorland that I wanted burnt-off: again, when the wind was away from the house.

I moved on to the farms which were an increasing joy. I toured them with Andrew Green and was pleased to find a motivated and happy bunch of people. I spoke with the farrier, the miller and the sawyer in charge of the saw mill. Everywhere I went I asked what I could do to improve the quality of their lives and I asked what they could do to make the Estate great again. Whether there were specific actions or no, all were committed to improving the enjoyment of our visitors. I felt I had their loyalty and support and I knew, as I had at the outset, that the problem had been at the centre.

On my return to the Manor I received a great piece of news. Oliver had returned. I welcomed him warmly and we spent an evening together, planning the forthcoming season.

The fishing season got under way and I devoted myself entirely to entertaining our guests, both on the river and back at the Manor. I was the first to rise each morning and the last to retire at night. Whilst avoiding obsequies, I treated each guest as my favourite friend and, with Oliver's assistance, fulfilled their every desire. It appeared to work and guests departed, full of praise for all they had experienced on the Estate.

Following the problems of the previous year, visitor numbers were reduced significantly. I spoke personally with every guest to identify any insult they had suffered last season. I made certain that, not only did they understand the cause but the understood that the cause had gone and we were working hard on their behalf to raise the Manor House Estate to even higher standards than before.

Each day I accompanied the parties to the river and patrolled back and forth, ensuring that each rod was happy with their stand and their gillie or other Estate support. It was hard work, but worthwhile and many a hurt from the previous year was forgotten and forgiven in our efforts that year.

However, the real medicine which was healing the horrors of the previous year was pride and confidence. Estate employees no longer lived in fear and dread for their livelihood at the possible retribution they might have suffered under Jonathan. Instead, they increasingly felt a sense of pride that we were indeed the best and that they personally could help make each one of our guests feel special. They rose to the challenge magnificently and I was thrilled at the results.

I had written a personal letter to each of our illustrious guests who normally joined us for the Glorious Twelfth and all but one turned up. The missing one was genuinely ill and promised to re-join us the following year. Oliver and I, and indeed all the workers on the Estate, worked hard to make the visit the very best they had experienced. They were amused that I was now the Laird and there were endless jokes bandying the titles Lord and Laird back and forth.

All the Estate workers continued to support our guests fully and each successive shoot passed off to my entire satisfaction. At the Harvest supper I was again able to make a speech. I reminded them that I had asked for their support and was able to thank them for giving it unstintingly.
"Since we set out on this journey in the spring, every single guest who has visited the Estate has enjoyed the experience. You have made each individual feel special and

appreciated. You have made each one feel that they were the most important visitor we have received. I want to thank you for your support and for making this happen. Our reputation was in danger and you, each one of you, has defended it to the hilt. Thank you."

There was tumultuous applause which I like to think was for themselves.

Chapter 22

The shoots continued unabated after the Harvest, through to Christmas and we had some excellent outings. Yes, numbers were still below previous years but the excellence of the sport and entertainment we gave our guests gave me every hope that numbers would increase next year through the recommendations of word of mouth.

I received a letter from John telling me that he just 'happened' to be travelling north to deal with a legal case and he thought that he might just 'happen' be in our area over Christmas; could he stay. I mentioned the letter to Morag and was rewarded with a most touching maidenly blush of happiness. I replied to the letter and bade him welcome.

I could see potential complications in the relationship of John and Morag. When he arrived two days before Christmas I took him aside for a fatherly talk. I told him I was happy with their friendship and would support him if it eventually led to a long-term relationship. However, I regarded Morag as my daughter and until he was certain of their long-term future I wished him to honour her chastity. John was a grown man and it was not an easy conversation but, so far as I am aware, he complied with my wishes. However, the two of them were never far from each other that holiday.

I also spoke with John about the education of the twins. Morag looked after the children well and had hitherto supplied some basic tuition and they could competently read and write but I needed to think what came next. I asked John his opinion on Richard going to the boarding school he had been at. He saw no objection except for the sadness of parting the twins who were very close. He wondered whether a better solution might be to secure the services of a scholarly tutor so that the two of them might be taught together. That sounded like an interesting solution and he promised to make enquiries, when he returned to London.

He left a few days after Christmas and I noticed that Morag had red, puffy rings around her eyes. There was clearly a wonderful attachment between them.

After his departure I sat down with Gregory to study the accounts of the Estate. The drop in the number of visitors had had a salutary effect on the income but, anticipating this, I had been most careful to avoid any unnecessary expenditure. As a result, we had generated a modest profit for the year. I anticipated that it would probably take three years to rebuild the number of visitors and I knew that I would need to continue to be careful and restrict cost increases to the activities which would directly benefit our guests.

I took one quarter of the profits from Gregory and together we rode across to The Chase. Jonathan was bed-bound and received us in his bedchamber. He was clearly a sick man and had the appearance of someone at death's door. He was not fit for extensive communication so we left the funds in the care of his secretary, and departed.

I knew that we had lost a number of house servants during Jonathan's tenure and discussed the situation with Grace. I emphasised that we needed to conserve funds until visitor numbers recovered but wished to explore where under-staffing might endanger guests' satisfaction. There were a couple of minor areas which needed bolstering but she felt that the household was running smoothly, particularly as guest numbers were lower than previously.

I had a similar conversation with Jason. He complained that he had neither a woodsman nor an assistant gamekeeper for the plot I had vacated beside the bend in the river and cheekily asked if I would like to continue to work that patch in my evenings. We had known each other for a long time now and I forgave him. I told him to re-staff that area and a few other areas where we were undermanned although we both knew that it might take some time to find suitable candidates.

As always, the shooting season continued unabated throughout January at which point our guests departed and we commenced the winter tasks such as rounding up the remaining game and enclosing them so that we could collect eggs for hatching game for the coming season. I took the opportunity to again visit every part of the Estate, urging everyone to complete any necessary work in preparation for the next season.

John wrote to tell me that he had found a candidate who he thought might be appropriate to tutor the twins. The fellow was a brilliant academic, skilled in mathematics, science, and classical languages. However, as sometimes happens with academics, he was completely impractical and had experienced difficulty in holding down a job. I felt that he sounded worth evaluating and wrote to John asking him to offer the man three months' work, following which we would decide whether to continue.

The tutor's name was Percival and he duly arrived and I had him installed in a room in which to school the children. He came to me after the first day to enquire whether I really wanted the girl (my daughter, Caitlin) to be educated. He clearly thought that education was wasted on women. I assured him that I did want her educated and set him a standard that I would like her to go to university when she attained the right age. Percival was a little scandalised by the suggestion but buckled down to his task.

In March, I received a message that Jonathan had suffered another stroke. I decided to visit him the following morning but, before I set out, I received another message to say that he had died in the night. I sent a letter to John and then made my way to The Chase to pay my respects; after all, we had once been friends. I took Gregory with me and asked him to prepare an inventory of everything in the house. I did this as a precaution to avoid things 'disappearing' before John could arrive.

Having paid my respects to the body I called for the housekeeper and secretary to join me in the lounge. I told them that my son, John, was the new owner of the Chase and would arrive in due time. In the meantime, they were to assume that they would all continue in his employ. I asked the secretary to produce to Gregory the accounts for The Chase.

The funeral would be at the chapel on the Manor House Estate and Jonathan would be laid to rest beside his parents and his bride. I asked them to urgently seek out the parson who had buried Elizabeth and organise a day for the burial. They were to let me know immediately when this had been agreed.

I felt a certain sadness as I rode away. Yes, we had once been friends and I had worked endlessly to make his Estate a profitable success. In one short year of madness he had ruined the work of years and had left me to be the owner of the problem. If only his mind had not been so damaged by the death of Elizabeth ……….. If only!

The funeral was organised for the following week and I made similar arrangements as those I had for Elizabeth. A grave for him was dug at her side and a guard of honour of Estate servants lined the pathway into the chapel, in their uniforms. The cortege arrived, accompanied by The Chase servants and the parson conducted the service and the burial. This time I was in charge and had asked Grace to prepare a wake meal in the Great Barn for the personnel from both estates. I had a feeling that the two estates would be working more closely together in future and it was a good opportunity for them to get to know each other.

John arrived from London two weeks later and we rode across to The Chase together. Through the secretary, Gregory had established that there were sufficient funds to keep the place operating for the current year and we would sit down at some stage and agree an arrangement for the future. I left him to get to know his staff and returned to the Manor House.

John arrived back at the Manor House a couple of days later, ostensibly to talk business although I was aware that the presence of Morag in our household might not have been wholly unconnected. I left them to have some time together before I became 'available' for our meeting.

When we finally sat down together I asked John if he had formed any plans for how he wanted to use The Chase. He told me that he had decided to live there and would like to try to build up income from sporting, in the same way as the Manor House. We were both fully aware that The Chase had costs to support, but currently had no regular income, save what they received from the Manor House Estate. However, that was not a totally honest summation as the Manor House received the income for the grouse shooting on The Chase land. We needed to find some way to apportion the profits equitably and I was confident that we could do that. For the rest of the season John wished to participate in each party of visitors so that he could develop his sporting skills and learn about the organisation and entertainment of guests.

We went on to discuss the twins' tutor, Percival. Although I was no scholar, I had paid close attention to their learning and they seemed to be progressing well under his instruction. I asked John to look-in on some of their classes so that we would be in a position to confirm Percival's appointment.

I was about to rise when John hurriedly interrupted saying "One other thing father. There is no one else to ask, so I would like to ask your permission to marry Morag. "

I was thrilled to hear this and replied that, if she would have him, he had my permission and my heart-felt blessing.

Morag apparently agreed and I congratulated them both and we were a happy family as we celebrated the twins' thirteenth birthdays a few days later. The youngsters were growing well. Sometimes it was still difficult to tell them apart and they delighted in the old trick of pretending each was the other one. But Richard was edging ahead in height and Caitlin had inherited the exquisite beauty and earth-shattering smile of her mother. I knew which was which.

As they had every year, they again invited some of their friends of the same age to join them. Whilst the youngsters played I broached the subject which was troubling me. Had John and Morag decided how the future of the twins would continue, following their marriage? They had obviously discussed the matter but wanted my views. They would be happy to take the children and their tutor to The Chase if I felt that best; alternatively, they could remain at the Manor House with a new nanny. I asked for time to consider that, before deciding.

Over the following weeks, John and I gradually worked out a programme for the two estates to work together. The Chase had only a short frontage of river so the opportunities for fishing were limited. However, there was a fairly substantial tarn behind the house which already held fish for use by the household. We agreed to stock that with additional fish from the hatchery to see if we could promote fishing there over a two or three-year period.

There were large herds of deer on some of the upper reaches of the estate and it would be possible to organise deer stalking. This could be profitable but only usually included one, or at the most two, guests at any one time. I offered the services of Yeoman Muckle to train up one of the gamekeepers to lead this sport.

The main asset of The Chase was the grouse moors. By now I regarded our illustrious guests who came each year for the opening shoot of the season as personal friends and I was reluctant to part with their company. The Manor House would host that event on the moorland which had been ceded to The Chase. All other grouse shoots on Chase lands would be organised and entertained by John and the income would belong to The Chase. Other shoots would be shared out, as appropriate.

The arrangement would deplete the apparent income of the Manor House Estate but, in reality, it was simply repositioning the costs of running The Chase which had formerly been taken from the coffers of the Estate. The total net costs or income had not changed. The changes did, however, inspire me to find new ways of driving up total income. I wrote again to every guest who had failed to appear in the past twelve months telling them that the Laird (the old Laird) had passed away and that we were now making both of the estates available to their sport. Marketing did not come to me naturally but I did my best to promote the estates and I was pleased when we received some positive responses and bookings.

Before the first party of fishermen arrived, I spent a day down at the farms in the company of Andrew Green. I shared with him the rather average financial result of the previous year and that it was about to worsen because John had rightly claimed the income which belonged to The Chase. What could he do to help increase our income?

As always, Andrew was on the ball. He had a number of plans which he wanted to advance. He had already established markets for all the excess production from the farms; beef, pork, poultry, flour and so on. He now wanted to expand the area of the farms by cutting down a sizeable area of woodland and turning it into farmland. The timber would create an immediate income and the increased farm area would produce additional output and income within a year. He had checked that the corn mill and the saw mill could cope with the additional throughput. I viewed the proposed area of land with him and approved the plan.

My discussion with Andrew sparked a thought in my head and, after testing the idea on him, I went to find Matthew Jamison, the Head Gillie. I knew that the quantity of fish in our river had grown significantly over recent years. After each day's fishing, most of the catch was normally returned to the river. I broached with him the idea that any salmon over a given size should be sent up to the smoke-house, rather than returned to the river. Smoked salmon could then be sent down to Andrew who was certain that he could find a market for it. Matthew was happy to agree the plan.

As the grass stopped growing in the fields each autumn and could no longer feed the larger animals, many were slaughtered. Some were hung on rafters inside the huge chimney flue from the kitchen fire to dry but the majority were packed in salt to preserve the meat through the winter months. Andrew's work in developing the use of winter crops to feed cattle had enabled us to retain larger numbers of animals alive through the winter. This meant that we could have fresh meat throughout and could also build-up our herds and flocks over time.

However, there was such an abundance of smaller game on the estate that we could usually snare it at any time of the year, as required, and we tended to be rather profligate with it. If there was a market for smoked fish, might there also be a market for smoked game?

I felt that I was on a roll and sought out Jason. We got through an enormous quantity of game each year, sometimes there was so much brought down in shoots that it went to waste. I asked him to send regular supplies of partridge, pheasant and venison to the smoke-house for treatment. It would then be sent down to Andrew who would organise its distribution into the market. Before heading for home, I had a quick look at the smokery. I had not examined it closely for years. It was old, but serviceable and should be able to cope with much increased volumes. I felt that we had identified a useful new form of income for the Estate.

Chapter 23

John and Morag announced that they would wed at Harvest time and I helped them plan an event which both the estates could celebrate. The wedding would be in the tiny chapel and, as we had now gone up in the world, we would secure the services of a parson and do the job properly. The reception would be in the Great Barn and everyone from both estates would be invited. I had still not answered the question of where the twins should live, after the wedding. I knew that if they went with the married couple to The Chase, they would be well looked after. But I also knew that I would miss them greatly. Since our return to the Manor House we had melded into a real family. The only way forward was to let the twins decide and I summoned them to my library and put the issue to them impartially. They were as indecisive as I was and argued the matter back and forth without coming to any conclusion. In the end I called a halt and told them to go away and talk about it and, when they had reached a decision, to let me know.

The fishing season commenced and it was good to welcome back friends, old and new. The fishing was excellent and I entertained our visitors royally in the Manor House each evening and I made certain that they enjoyed their stay. Some good-sized salmon and trout were pulled from the river and sent to the smoke-house, on the way to new markets.
I reviewed activity at the smoke-house and found that it was working well. Whereas it had often operated nearly empty, it was now bursting with Estate produce and Andrew had identified markets for our goods and was confident he could sell all we could produce. The whole activity was generating a lively income for the Estate. I was pleased and decided to allocate an Estate worker to operate it on a full-time basis and maximise the output.

Each fishing event was better supported than the last and it was clear that the numbers of visitors were up on the previous year. We were gaining ground and the comments from guests convinced me that we were increasingly achieving our objective of 'excellence'. As the year moved on I insisted that John should closely involve himself with Jason in the planning of the autumn shoots so that he gained experience for organising events on The Chase. He also joined me on many evenings at the dinners at which we entertained our guests. He was a lively conversationalist and I was confident that he would make a good host.

The twins came to me rather shyly one afternoon and announced that they had made their decision on their future. They would like to stay with John and Morag at The Chase. They seemed embarrassed at having chosen to leave me but I assured them it was all right. They had spoken with John and Morag and had agreed on the introduction of a new family tradition. After the wedding we would always try to meet together for Sunday lunch as a family. It was a nice idea and I happily agreed.

August arrived and I prepared for the Glorious Twelfth. I had claimed it as my own but I invited John to be part of the party as he might well wish to host his own gatherings in future years. Our distinguished guests arrived and together we entertained them to the pre-shoot dinner. Having lived in London, John was far more able than I to enter into parts of the conversation which were as a foreign language to me. We dined and wined long into the night.

As usual, we were up before dawn and let the bumps of the horse-drawn omnibus conveyance shake off our hang-overs as we made our way up onto the grouse moors. The beaters approached from the far side of the moor and we had an excellent mornings sport. John had recently acquired a shotgun and turned out to be a credible shot. He clearly had a good eye.

We had laid on a special luncheon for the occasion. In addition to the usual fare, Grace had included a selection of the various delicacies of our own smoked produce and some excellent malt whisky to compliment them. The repast was extremely popular and the guests refused to budge until the platter was empty. The whisky was similarly popular but many grouse that should have fallen that afternoon, lived to fly another day as a result of the effects of the malt whisky.

Notwithstanding, it had been a most enjoyable day and we had a respectable, if not record bag. We journeyed home on the omnibus conveyance in great frivolity and adjourned to the paved courtyard for pre-prandial drinks and tales of the grouse which managed to dodge five barrel-loads of shot. We drank to him and wished him well.

The dinner that evening excelled with the most exotic fare we could muster. Our guests were impressed and were kind enough to remark that we had made a strong recovery from the problems we had experienced under Jonathan. I shared with them the fact that we had lost many visitors as a result of Jonathan's illness and they each offered to promote the Manor House to their friends and acquaintances. They were as good as their word and we had a number of new guests over the following year.

Following the departure of those guests I divided my time between entertaining subsequent parties and helping John to entertain the parties on The Chase. He had been thorough in his preparation and the grouse shoots on his land were highly successful. It was interesting to share in his entertainment at his house, The Chase. Jonathan had spared no cost when refurbishing the place for his bride and it was certainly a splendid venue for the shoot dinners. Many of those taking part had formerly been guests at the Manor House and I was anxious to ensure that they were happy with the new location. It was smaller than the Manor House and seemed to generate a greater intimacy for the parties. I felt slightly superfluous and decided that I would in future only appear by specific invitation.

Harvest was fast approaching and, with it, the wedding day. I had awarded all personnel the Saturday off with the exception of kitchen servants and dairy farmers. John and I had agreed to combine the wedding feast with the Harvest supper and throw a party the like of which had not been seen on either of our estates. We would start with a celebration luncheon after the wedding ceremony and would continue through until night-time. The parson had been booked and the chapel was filled with flowers and harvest produce, all was ready.

I escorted Morag from the Manor House. She was radiant and looked incredibly beautiful as we rode in the pony and trap to the chapel. John was already there waiting for her. The line-up for the wedding was perhaps as bizarre as could possibly be conceived. My daughter, Caitlin, was bridesmaid for her nurse. My son, Richard was groom's man for his half-step brother. I, the step-father of the groom acted as surrogate father to the bride and gave the nurse away to my step-son. Confusing, but it worked. The ceremony was beautiful and I cried although I know not if it was for my step-son or for Morag or because neither Mary nor Caitlin could be present. But the tears were tears of happiness.

After the ceremony we processed together from the chapel, down to the Great Barn in the sunshine. Many from the Estate had already assembled there and there was a huge cheer as the bride and groom entered. And then we partied. It went on for the rest of the day and I was too happy and too befuddled to remember much of the details. It was a great occasion. I do recall that, shortly before darkness fell we loaded the bride and groom onto the pony and trap and they left for their new home at The Chase, accompanied by a party of Chase employees, bearing burning torches.

Caitlin and Richard would join them a few days later but for now, I led them back to the Manor House and to their beds. It had been a wonderful day.

John had not arranged any fixtures at The Chase for the next ten days but guests arrived at the Manor House on the Monday. I recovered from the excitement of the wedding and welcomed them and feted them as though they were the only guests in our entire calendar.

Excellence and attention to detail had become our watchwords and their visit was a success, as was every subsequent one on our Estate and also on The Chase. We were good at what we did and guests did indeed feel honoured and valued and that they had been accorded every courtesy.

It was clear that our pursuit of excellence was working. Numbers of visitors were gradually recovering and this represented a welcome increase in revenues although some of the income from them belonged to The Chase. Equally pleasing was the fact that we had received a good increase from timber sales and from the farm surplus. We had also generated an excellent income from our smoked products. This promised to be a strong source of income for the future.

Christmas was approaching once more and I was in a quandary on how to stage it. The easy answer would have been to insist that John, Morag and the twins spend the day at the Manor House and take part in the traditions there. Common sense told me that they needed to be together at The Chase and to start to invent their own traditions in their new home. As a result, I felt a loneliness and sadness as I handed out gifts to the children at the Manor House that Christmas morn. I felt empty and devoid and I missed Caitlin's hand in mine as we processed down to the Great Barn. I invited Grace and Gregory to join me at the top table at dinner, but in my mind, I was alone. I felt a sadness and loneliness that Christmas without my family around me. The wheel of time had turned and, to a large extent, my work as a husband and a father was done. I was superfluous.

January brought heavy snow. Our shooting parties continued but the going was heavy. Guests traipsed through the snow to the shoots, only to find that the game lay snug in their nests and unless one was actually about to stand on them, they were reluctant to budge. As shoots, they were not particularly successful. Nonetheless, we balanced this with making a superb effort with the level of the entertainment we lavished on our guests and, with Oliver's careful attention to detail, we had some great parties.

<u>Chapter 24</u>

With the New Year, a change came over me; it was a continuation of the emotions I had experienced on Christmas Day. I was feeling tired and I had lost my spark and enthusiasm for life. I had established that the finances were improving and I knew without doubt that the year just starting would be better still but I had lost my drive. In part I knew that it was because John, Morag and the twins were no longer part of my daily life and I missed having them around me. But also, I was growing old. I had twice rescued the Estate from financial ruin and felt a moderate pleasure in that but I could not find the enthusiasm to drive forward, either for the Estate or for myself. I was lonely and depressed.

I neglected my duties and took myself off to my childhood home where I sat on the bench and shivered as I watched my river. I wanted to rest, to abrogate my responsibilities, I wanted peace. Mesmerised by the movement of the river and by the murmur of its siren song, I felt my eyes start to close and a drowsiness came upon me as I watched. For the first time in my life, I willed the river to carry me with it, far, far away to its destination in a void of sweet oblivion. It would not accept me into that sweet nothingness.

Just as I was on the point of drifting into sleep I heard my father's voice, loud and clear.
"Come Richard, there is more work to be done".
I awoke with a start.
He was right. Over a hundred souls on the Estate relied on me for their livelihood and their daily bread and my job was not yet finished.

I sprang to my feet, electrified and renewed and retraced my steps back to the Manor House. Jason had taken a shooting party into a nearby part of the forest. I quickened my step and soon came upon them. I spent the rest of the day giving them my undivided attention as their perfect and attentive host.

The sound of my father's voice and his clear admonition galvanised me back into the real world and I worked as a man possessed. Throughout January I devoted myself to our guests and ensuring that they lacked for nothing. And when the last of the shoots left at the end of the month I threw myself into a minute examination of every part of the Estate and every activity thereupon.

I wrote to Miss Tamsin Grey and invited her to visit us once again to give us the benefit of her keen and imaginative eye to make suggestions on how we might raise our standards further still in the interests of our guests. She kindly accepted my invitation and arrived at the Manor at the beginning of February. It had been three years since her last visit and I brought her up to date on changes since then. I had explained in my letter that I did not envisage major works on the same scale as on the last occasion but I would value any ideas that might occur to her and would reimburse her for her time.

We spent a long time wandering from room to room through the Manor House. Tamsin had a brilliant eye for detail and came up with endless ideas for improving the general ambience of the house. Many ideas were fairly minor although together they would help to create a greater impression of opulence. One of the larger ideas which I particularly liked was to replace the rather mundane stairs in the front hall with a magnificent, sweeping staircase which divided half way up with separate staircases continuing to either side to the upper landing. I could envisage it and it would hugely enhance the appearance and grandeur of the hall.

We spent a number of hours together discussing various ideas and I suddenly realised that I was enjoying her company and I looked at her properly for the first time. She was slim and held herself very upright; her hair was tied in a tidy bun at the back of her head. Her clothes were of good quality but were simple and unadorned, accentuating the impression of a rather severe demeanour. I looked carefully into her face and saw that she was still an attractive woman and I guessed that she was perhaps ten years younger than I. On our last meeting I had thought her lacking in humour but I realised that she had made a number of amusing comments as we had toured the house this morning.

We took a light luncheon together in the dining room whilst we continued to discuss various ideas for the house and, on an impulse; I invited her to tour part of the Estate with me. We went first to visit the farms and I introduced her to Andrew Green who regaled us with his latest plans for the area. Once again, Tamsin produced a host of little suggestions for a wide variety of situations. I think that both Andrew and I were humbled as we listened to her good, common-sense ideas.

It was getting dark as we left Andrew and drove the pony and trap back up 'Jack's Highway'. I noticed Tamsin fall silent and then realised that she had dozed into sleep and was resting her head against my shoulder. I could smell her perfume and it was intoxicating. I slowed the pony to a walk to make the moment last as long as possible and was disappointed when the Manor House hove into view all too soon. Tamsin awoke and gave me a gentle peck on the cheek before I alighted and helped her down. The moment had passed.

We had already arranged that she would stay the night and one of the maids showed her to her room. Later, we again dined together and, as the meal ended I summoned the courage to speak what was on my mind.
"Miss Grey; or Tamsin if I may call you that, I have greatly enjoyed your company today and, if you will forgive me, I

find you most attractive. It is none of my business, but I would love to learn more about you and your life, if you would care to tell me."

"Thank you, Richard." She replied. "I have enjoyed your company too and I greatly admire what you are trying to achieve on this estate." And she went on to tell me a little of her life story. She had been born into money and had lived in a house not dissimilar to the Manor House. Her mother had died when she was young and her father had later invested unwisely in a shipping venture to the southern seas and had lost his entire fortune. They had moved to meagre rented accommodation and the shame had driven him to drink and an early grave. She had been betrothed to a young man who had deserted her when he learned that the family fortune was lost. She realised that she had a talent for interior design and had used her contacts to secure some business although she feared that this source was now running dry.

I thanked her and told her of my humble beginnings and how the wheel of fortune had carried me to the present lofty heights. We talked long into the night and, before we retired, I told her I had already decided to go ahead with her idea for the staircase. I asked if she thought it might be possible to complete it before our first guests started arriving in early April. It was a tough request, but I left her to think it over. I slept in later than usual the following morning and, when I arose, I found Tamsin already making measurements and sketches for the staircase.

Before she left, I invited her to join me in a tour of the Estate Office and the Great Barn. Once again she had an endless fund of little ideas for enhancing the appearance and functionality of each area. We looked at the row of Estate cottages. Since the refurbishment three years ago they looked neat and presentable. However, with a woman's eye, Tamsin noted that the recent rains had churned the pathway in front of them into a muddy quagmire, through which each person had to wade to and from their home. Why did we not drain and surface it? It was such eminently sensible observations as this that made me admire her knowledge and ability.

I gave immediate instructions for a ditch to be dug on the far side of the path to drain the water. Later, when the path had dried somewhat, I had cartloads of sawdust brought up from the saw mill to help drain and bind the soil. Later still, cartloads of chippings were brought from the quarry to provide a surface.

We parted later that morning and I saw Tamsin off in her pony and trap. She promised to talk with some woodworking experts she knew and, if they were available, to send them in my direction. I thanked her and, looking into her eyes, I asked that she would return with them to oversee the work. I wanted to see more of her; much more. For the first time in a long while, I felt a sense of happiness.

After Tamsin had departed I sought out Matthew Jamison to discuss plans for the forthcoming fishing season. I was delighted to hear that bookings for the current season were significantly increased. He told me that the programme was now full and he was having to reject any further applications. I asked him not to reject them but to give them to me. I would write to the applicants offering the alternative of the new tarn facility on The Chase estate. The ploy worked well and I was able to hand on several dozen applications to John to help him build up his income.

Whilst we had been down with Andrew I had quizzed him about the way forward for smoked products. It had gone well and I wanted to see if we could increase significantly our sales. I asked him to enquire about pack sizes, portion sizes, packaging and presentation. He agreed to do so and, predictably, Tamsin had chimed in with a raft of good ideas.

I also sought views from Grace although her comments were slanted towards catering for sizeable households.

Andrew researched the subject in depth with the customers he supplied and some useful ideas emerged. We made changes and the demand continued to grow. I could foresee that we would need to increase the size of the smoke-house, ere too long.

About a fortnight after her departure, Tamsin's carpenters arrived with cartloads of timber. Before allowing them to proceed I took their boss aside and made it clear that the work had to be completed by the end of March. If he did not think he could achieve that, I did not wish him to start. The man was confident he could achieve that date and I allowed him to commence. Day after day the house was filled with the sound of sawing and banging and, for at least a week, the only way to bed was up a ladder.

Whilst the work continued, Tamsin returned and I confess that I was delighted to see her again. She took over as clerk of works and my presence to oversee and expedite the work on the staircase became entirely unnecessary. She harangued the men, day and night.

We dined together most evenings and our conversations became increasingly relaxed and informal. One evening she addressed me saying "Richard, I have another project for you. All the water for the Manor House has to be pumped by hand from the well. It has to be distributed by hand in buckets, not just within the kitchens, but to every bedroom where it is then poured from the jug into a basin for washing."

"In many cities, water is now piped into houses and distributed throughout the building by water pipes to each room with a faucet to start and stop the flow. I have been looking at the possibility for here. I believe that we could channel water from a little way up the river with sufficient force to raise it to a tank in the roof space. From there, we could pipe it into the kitchens and to each bedroom and guests would have an endless supply of fresh water." She paused to gauge my reaction.

I thought it a revolutionary idea and said I would like it fully appraised and an estimate of cost produced. I did, however, make one stipulation. If we proceeded then I must insist that she remained here to oversee the work. She agreed.

As we discussed the concept, three issues emerged.

The first was that, whilst the channelling, the tank and possibly the supply to the kitchen could proceed throughout the year, piping to the individual bedrooms would need to await the period in the spring when we were without visitors.

The second was that we would also need to devise some method of drainage to remove used water from the rooms.

The third was that we were going to need a significant length of lead pipe to achieve the project.

We agreed that these issues were not insurmountable, but needed to be investigated.

We sat at the table, side by side, long into the night turning over ideas and plans. At one point I allowed my hand to touch, caress and hold Tamsin's hand. She permitted the intimacy for a minute or more then lifted her hand and mine to her lips, kissed my hand and released the hold.

Chapter 25

The end of March loomed large and the arrival of our guests in early April could not be delayed. Would the staircase be completed on time?

With Tamsin at the helm I should not have doubted for one moment. She had more power than the water wheel driving the mill and I was certain that the workmen had concluded it would be safer for them to cut their own throats rather than risk her wrath if they were late in completing their task.

Miraculously, the timberwork was completed two-thirds of the way through the month and they spent the remainder of the time sanding, staining and varnishing their work.

The result was truly outstanding. In his irrational period, Jonathan might well have burnt the entire house down to express his horror at the profligacy of the construction. But it was wonderful and imposing and I was certain our guests would appreciate the opulence and eloquence of the work as they ascended to their rooms.

When at last it was complete and the workmen had departed I opened a bottle of champagne and shared it with Tamsin. We walked up and down the staircase together, toasting each step and wishing it long life and stability. We retired to the dining room and enjoyed each other's conversation as we dined. We talked about the water project and I reminded Tamsin that if we were to proceed, I would insist upon her continued presence. She rose from her chair and came to stand beside me.

"Richard, I have been badly let down in my past and, if I am to stay here for some time, I shall shortly need to ask you if your intensions are honourable."

I looked into her face and smiled saying "No, my intentions towards you are entirely dishonourable." She blushed and I continued, "But if you mean to ask if I will marry you, then my thoughts are moving very much in that direction. Give me a few more weeks and I will hope to give you an honest answer."

Tamsin bent and kissed me on the lips saying "thank you," then retired to her bed without another word.

I sent a note to The Chase telling John that I would like an invitation to the twin's fourteenth birthday party. I added that Miss Tamsin Grey, the interior decoration expert, was staying at the Manor House and would he have any objection if she joined me. He replied with a formal invitation for us both. We drove across in a pony and trap and had a most delightful evening with the family. The twins still enjoyed party games but they were becoming increasingly sophisticated and grown up. I enjoyed the spectacle of them all looking at me and then at Tamsin and trying to work out if this was more than a business relationship. I left them in the dark. Tamsin was the life and soul of the party with her stories and anecdotes. The conversation was easy and I could tell that the family warmed to her. We enjoyed an excellent dinner together and it was wonderful to see the happiness on the faces of Morag and John. The twins too seemed very happy and contented.

The twins left us for a brief period to pursue other interests and, whilst they were gone, John told me that he had commissioned a small extension to the stable block. The workmen had created a new access to the extension and, in the process, had discovered a small hidden chamber. In it were the skeletons of two adults and a child. I recalled immediately Jonathan's comment about the mysterious disappearance of some members of the family. The event would have taken place before Caitlin was born but it seemed likely that she knew about it and that it had been the cause of her unwillingness ever to return to the Chase.

If the housekeeper knew of the incarceration, it was possible that she might have used it as a threat to control Caitlin when she was little but, if she had any hand in the affair, she had taken that knowledge with her to the grave. It was history and there was little point in pursuing the matter. No one remained who might be able to enlighten us as to their demise.

At the end of the evening Tamsin and I climbed back into the trap and set-off for the Estate. It was a beautiful moonlit night and half way home I brought the pony to a halt. I turned to Tamsin saying "I did tell you that my intentions towards you were entirely dishonourable," I pulled her towards me and kissed her, long and hard. She responded fully and warmly and I continued for as long as decency would allow before pulling away.

As I flicked the reigns to drive the pony forward again I heard her whisper "I think I rather like your dishonourable intentions. Oh! And by the way, I like your family too."

A few days later the fishing season commenced and with it the requirement for me to attend each event and to entertain our guests each evening. Everyone who entered the Manor House was truly impressed with the new staircase and it became a talking point. I had reinstated Oliver's desk adjacent to the foot of the stairs and he sat there proudly orchestrating our comings and goings and organising us all.

I had warned Tamsin that I would be involved in entertaining guests on many evenings over the next few months and she was not to think that I was neglecting her. I asked her to proceed with evaluating the ideas for the piped water system and that occupied a considerable amount of her time that spring. Whenever I had a spare evening I would spend it with her and I also devoted most of my weekends to her. Since our pony-ride in the moonlight, it transpired that, like Caitlin, she rather enjoyed kissing. We practised many times but I was careful to keep within the bound or propriety and did not venture further. I enjoyed the intimacy of kissing her although I knew that the bolt of lightning which had always flown instantly between Caitlin and myself, was absent. I put this down to the fact that we were both older.

I knew, however, that I needed to make a decision for both our sakes and I was undecided. I was mulling this over in my mind one morning when I walked back into the Manor. Tamsin was at the front desk with Oliver and there was obviously an altercation in progress. I enquired as to the cause and Oliver told me apologetically that he had let Miss Grey down. She was unhappy with her room and had asked to be moved but, until our guests left on Friday, there was not a single other room he could relocate her to.

I replied that the matter was easily resolved. He should move her into the master bedroom until another room became available and move my effects to the room she had occupied.

I went on to say that they had highlighted a growing problem. With the increasing numbers of guests, we were often now short of rooms. I recalled that both the twin's old nursery and the schoolroom had been left as such and asked Oliver to organise for them to be refurbished and brought into service as a guest rooms.

The fishing season had got off to a good start. The river was in spate which added to the excitement and challenge for the rods and despite the conditions every visitor managed to land a credible catch each day. They had thoroughly enjoyed the sport.

We were having a hilarious time at the dinner table one evening recounting tales of the excitement of the day. The atmosphere was friendly and convivial when I suddenly became aware of raised voices in the small dining room at the rear of the house. I prided myself that raised voices were rare since I had returned to the Manor House so I excused myself and made my way to the room. There was a blazing row in progress between Tamsin and Grace. It transpired that Tamsin was angry because she felt she was being ignored and was receiving poor service whilst the staff pandered to the needs of my party of guests. I apologised to Tamsin, whilst reminding her that our visitors paid for the running of the Estate. I asked Grace if it might be possible for one of the maids to be dedicated to attending to Miss Grey's needs whilst the other servants served our guests.

In bed that night I pondered upon these incidents and suddenly realised that there had been several more over recent weeks. The matter came to a head on Saturday evening when Tamsin and I were dining alone. One of the serving girls was a little clumsy and Tamsin immediately flew off the handle at her. The maid rushed from the room in a flood of tears. Tamsin looked embarrassed at what she had done and apologised to me but the incident had crystallised my thoughts. This was not going to work.

I told Tamsin that I was still not in a position to decide on our future and I desired a cooling-off period in which to reach an answer. I asked that she return to her home for a month and I would write to tell her my decision at the end of that time. If I invited her back, it would be with the clear understanding that we would wed.

I organised for Gregory to pay Miss Grey handsomely for her work with us and for her ideas. The following morning we loaded Tamsin and her possessions into her pony and trap. She was tearful, but I was resolute. I needed time to think.

I was sad when she had gone because I had enjoyed her company, as well as her swift mind and endless clever ideas. I had also enjoyed the opportunity to kiss a woman once more. At the same time, I knew that it was the right decision. My experience with Jonathan's mental illness following the death of Elizabeth had armed me against ever again allowing conflict and unreasonable behaviour to enter my house. I also recognised beyond doubt that the harmony and deep love I had experienced with Caitlin was not present in my relationship with Tamsin. I waited for a month before writing to Tamsin telling her, as kindly and gently as I could, that I did not feel in a position to propose marriage to her and believed it wrong to allow her hopes in that direction to continue.

I immersed myself into the routine of my daily duties and let them absorb me and force me to look forward, not back. I implemented many new innovations across the Estate, including some that had been proposed by Tamsin. I liked her suggestion of running water in the house but did not yet feel ready to move that forward.

One thing was certain; the number of visitors was steadily increasing. This was precisely the result we sought and we had no difficulty in handling the numbers on the Estate. However, without doubt it placed pressure on the availability of bedrooms and I increasingly had to vacate the master bedroom to accommodate some guest or other. On more than one occasion I slept on the chaise longue in the lounge so that every visitor had their own bed chamber.

The idea of extending the Manor House was starting to formulate in my mind and I made enquiries of several of our guests seeking not only a reputable builder, but also experts experienced in indoor water systems. The idea of a new west wing was born. My enquiries with guests paid off and I was able to identify and engage reputable contractors and to progress designs for the new accommodation.

I resolved that the accommodation would be of the very highest standard, designed to raise the reputation of the Estate to new heights. Each room would have an en-suite water closet with a washbowl fed with fresh water through a faucet. There would be a commode drained to the outside and there would be a hip-bath for guests to bathe. I hoped that we might eventually be able to pipe hot water to this although initially I had no idea how this might be achieved.

Work on the culvert to bring water from the river started during the summer and, for the most part, the works were not really apparent to our guests. Similarly, I had hurdles erected to hide work on the foundations of the new building from sight. By the early autumn the basic structure was complete, the roof was in place and work had commenced on the internal fittings. I was fascinated by the work of the water engineers. They were called plumbers, apparently after the Latin for the lead they used for their pipes. The culvert and piping proved ample to provide the pressure to raise the river water to a tank installed in the roof of the new building. The pipes snaked throughout the building from there, delivering fresh water to every location.

I talked with their leader at length on how we might also be able to introduce heated water to the rooms. He told me it was well known that hot water would rise inside a pipe. We made various designs and experimented with trying to raise heated water to a second tank in the roof space. It worked and with increasing ingenuity, we managed to distribute the heated water to the hip-baths. We had seemingly achieved the impossible.

In the meantime, the normal events of the year continued. Our illustrious guests for the Glorious Twelfth were all present this year and they eulogised over the magnificence of the new grand staircase and declared that it added significantly to the general aura of the Manor House.

As we sat round the table after the shoot, eating the first grouse which had sacrificed itself in the interests of the Estate, I shared with them the plans for the new wing. There were mixed views on the wisdom of bringing water within a building but there was general agreement that it was bold and innovative. They would look forward to trying it next year.

The shoots continued, punctuated by the Harvest supper and I was particularly mindful that year of how bountiful the Harvest had been from every activity on the Estate. When I finally sat down with Gregory at the end of the year to review our results, I was rewarded with the discovery that it had been our most profitable year ever. Despite the money I was spending on the new wing, our funds were strong. I checked to ensure that the income for The Chase was also performing well. It was less stellar than for the Estate, but income was exceeding their costs.

I was honour-bound to fulfil the Christmas Day traditions of the Manor House and with help from Grace, presents were organised for every child on the Estate. Whilst they were opening them and playing I dispensed generous Christmas spirit to every adult and we sang carols together around the huge Christmas tree. Afterwards we processed together down to the Great Barn and feasted, danced and celebrated long into the night. On the following day, Boxing Day, I invited myself to lunch at The Chase and we had a wonderful family party. It was enhanced by the news from John and Morag that Morag was expecting a baby. I had no idea what my official relationship with the babe would be. Suffice for me was the news of the expected arrival and I was happy to position myself as an expectant grandfather.

My own children, Richard and Caitlin, were nearing adulthood. They had prospered well under their tutor, Percival, and were starting to talk in terms of possible studies at university. The two of them were full of life and bursting with energy and it was a joy to share time with them.

Replete from my meal, I sat dozing in front of the fire as the excitement carried on around me and I thought of the twists and turns my life had taken since that day, long ago, when I had pulled from the river, that sodden bundle which contained John.

Should I have thrown it back? I thought not; but how much water had flowed down my river since.

<u>Chapter 26</u>

The New Year brought new challenges as well as repeated ones. The west wing was finally completed at the end of February. I toured each room and played with the marvel of the water system, turning each faucet on and off. The hot water system had caused problems and some occasional flooding, but now it was working well. Hot water was piped from behind the kitchen range, to a holding tank in the roof space. The water tended to cool rather quickly in the tank, but we gradually improved the efficiency of the system.

As the builders finished on the west wing, I redirected them to erect several new workers cottages and a new manager's house which I felt I might need. I also arranged for the water engineers to return the following spring to install water closets in the older bedrooms.

The twins celebrated their fifteenth birthday and I was pleased to be invited to join them and to attend. They were no longer children but developing adults and John and Morag had instilled into them excellent manners and graces. I was proud of them.

The first guests started to arrive for the fishing season and they were most impressed with the luxury of the new west wing. I know that many of them played with the faucets as I had, turning them on and off. Some, who may only rarely have bathed in the past, took advantage of the hip baths and the hot water to luxuriate in, after their fishing trip.

Numbers of guests rose continually and we occasionally had to press some of the older rooms back into service to the disappointment of those who missed out on the luxury of the new rooms in the west wing.

In July, Morag produced a son and she and John were so proud of the bairn, as was its doting grandfather. They called him John, which seemed good to me.

In August our traditional guests arrived for the Glorious Twelfth and, like everyone else, they eulogised over the luxury of their new rooms. Over dinner they decided as a body that they wished to stay an extra night next year, just to be able to use the bath again.

More shoots followed and more satisfied guests, and then it was Harvest time once more with all the traditions that came with it. Three more months of shoots and it was Christmas again and the turn of another year.

I was starting to feel my age. I took a decision to have a thorough review of the managers on the Estate with a view to reducing my own workload.

I started inside the Manor House. Oliver, who had brilliantly smoothed the organisation of our events, still had plenty of life in him. Gregory was nearing retirement age. I had recruited an assistant for him some time ago but Jonathan had immediately dismissed him as superfluous. I talked the matter through with Gregory and told him that, if he wished to contemplate retirement in the next few years, I required him to recruit and train his successor. He found an appropriate individual and the process worked well.

I had a long discussion with Grace on how she would like to see things develop in her kingdom. She was not yet ready to contemplate retirement but was aware of the pressures of continually increasing numbers of guests and we agreed a number of changes to ease her work load.

Matthew Jamison asked me for two more people to help support our visitors as they fished. I was unwilling to agree to add two more gillies who would spend most of the year walking up and down the river banks but we discussed his requirements and identified productive roles for them which would still allow them to be available to support the rods.

Jason was quite a number of years older than I and I knew that he would be contemplating retirement in a few years' time. I was still impressed with young Dale Watler and I knew that, as overseer, he was already doing much of the day-to-day recruiting and organisation for the shooting parties. I had a similar conversation as that with Gregory to impress on Jason that he must train Dale to be his replacement, before he could contemplate retirement. Since inheriting The Chase, John had taken over the management of his gamekeepers there so the task was a little reduced. Against this, we had increased the number of assistant gamekeepers on our estate and the increasing intensity of shoots kept him fully occupied.

This left the question of an Estate Manager. I needed someone who was forward thinking and could not only embrace change, but could instigate and drive it. He also needed the ability to take his people with him in the process. I knew just the right man.

I rode down to see Andrew Green at the farms and found him surrounded by an ever-growing number of children. I told him that he clearly had far too much time on his hands and he needed a proper job. Would he be interested in the job of Estate Manager and, if so, how would we manage the farms?

He was certainly interested and tremendously excited by the possibility of the challenge. He told me that the farms were now fully organised and well under control, which I knew to be correct. He went on to add that he had been training one of the farmers to act as overseer and he was showing plenty of talent in that role. Andrew was confident that he could continue to manage farm activity remotely, through his overseer. I asked him to talk it over with his wife and come to see me later in the week.

He was on my doorstep two mornings later. He was buzzing with excitement, ideas and questions; he was up for it. He was fully conversant with the farm area so I decided to accompany him on a tour of the rest of the Estate so that I could try to see it through his eyes. He did not disappoint me. Wherever we went he noticed things of importance, he contributed ideas and made entirely sensible and pertinent comments. When we finally returned to the Manor House I showed him the changes there since his last visit including the magnificent staircase and the water closets in the bedrooms. He was impressed.

We sat in the library to discuss the role of the Estate Manager and what I required of him. He was perfectly comfortable with my demands and I went on to tell him the remuneration for the job. Finally, before he left, I took him to inspect the new managers house I had had built in anticipation of this appointment. Suffice to say that he was thrilled and a few days later he arrived with a wagon loaded with all his family and effects.

This all left me with just one remaining role; that of accompanying our guests on their shooting or fishing trips and entertaining them on something approaching two hundred nights each year. I was on first name terms with many of our guests and was happy to continue the task for a few more years but I knew that I needed to find someone to assume the work for the future. John was the obvious candidate and I went to discuss the matter with him although it also gave me an excellent opportunity to visit my grandson and the twins.

We had not really discussed progress on The Chase for some time, nor John's hopes and aspirations for the future. He was enjoying his life as the Squire of his estate. The

Chase was generating a modest income but he knew he needed some additional sources of income for the future.

As John had already inherited The Chase I told him that it was my wish that the twins should inherit the ownership of the Manor House Estate when I died. However, to even things up, John should be entitled to one third of the profits of the Estate during his lifetime, if he was prepared to gradually assume the task of accompanying and entertaining our visitors. He was perfectly amenable to that and started to take up his duties almost immediately.

With the increasing numbers of visitors, we occasionally found that we were each hosting a separate reception on the same night, but there were also increasing opportunities when I could absent myself and leave the task in John's capable hands.

I was pleased with my review of the Estate and was confident that our machine would now run smoothly for the future.

And so, another year turned, and another, and another and another.

The twins were at university together. John and I had had to pull a number of strings and endow a chair at the college to enable young Caitlin to be admitted at the same time as her brother, Richard, but it was worth it. They were still inseparable, studying mathematics, science and engineering; the last of which I felt would stand them in good stead, should they decide to take up estate management. My grandson, John was already growing into a real character and I spent increasing time with him.

And I was growing old.

I found myself increasingly wracked by coughs and colds, aches and pains and illnesses. I told John that I no longer felt fit or able to host our guests and left the matter entirely to him.

I felt uncomfortable occupying the huge Master Bedroom in the great Manor House. It was cold and lonely and I moved out to one of the little Estate cottages although I was pleased to find the Andrew had now had water supplied directly to each one. Grace very kindly had a meal sent round each day from her kitchens and I lacked for nothing.

My health was deteriorating and I seemed to experience increasing pains in my chest. I had enjoyed excellent health in my working career and it irritated me to feel that I was becoming an invalid. I was a shrunken shell of my former self. I knew that there were increasing periods when I did not move from the fireside for days on end and, in truth, I no longer cared.

As old men do, I sat and thought on times past. I thought of all that had taken place over the years and what I had achieved, against all odds. I thought of my family, John and Morag and of my twins and grandson. I thought of my former Laird, Jonathan and how his illness had caused so much damage and how it had finally brought security for the future of my family. I thought of my two lovely wives, Mary and Caitlin and the love I had shared with them. I thought of my father and how his diligent and patient instruction had helped me in my work. I thought of the tiny cottage he had built near the island in the river, just where it turns eastwards and I longed to see it once more.

I called for a pony and trap to be brought to my cottage and I set off to have one last look at my childhood home.

Chapter 27

Have you ever sat and watched a river or listened to its song? I had, many times.

I was feeling quite unwell as I reached my old home and climbed painfully down from the trap. Like myself, the old bench was looking decidedly rickety, but it held and I sat there and watched my river once more and listened to its song as it chuckled, gurgled and bounced care-free across the stones. The song was friendly, welcoming, inviting.

The pain in my chest had worsened as I travelled and I sat very still, waiting for it to pass.

I gazed at the flowing river, willing it to wash away my pain in its headlong rush towards eternity; knowing that no single droplet of water would ever pass this way again.

The thought of eternity caused me to dwell upon my own destiny.
Would St Peter admit me through the gates of Heaven? I hoped so.
I had wronged no man nor had I mistreated any woman.
I had sought to live a decent life; to live it soberly and to treat everyone with courtesy, kindness and compassion. Would that be sufficient?

A stab of lightening knifed through my chest again and I winced in pain.

I had enjoyed a good life with opportunities and blessings beyond my wildest dreams although even now I was not certain what barque of fortune had borne me thence. I had taken two loving wives, Mary and Caitlin and I longed to see them both again in paradise. My real hope was that I could spend eternity with Caitlin. Would that be allowed? How would Mary feel?

I hoped that we could work something out.

The pain in my chest was becoming excruciating; I bent over to try to ease it but it would not go. I felt the siren song of the waters of my river calling me, drawing me as it flowed on and on towards oblivion: it promised me peace, gentleness, calm; an end to pain and strife.

I felt myself falling, falling, falling ....

THE END